I0684928

THE CITY

KAREEM HICKS

Please e-mail Kareem Hicks at kareemhicksthecity@gmail.com with any feedback. Your comments are very much appreciated

www.kareemhicks.com

Book covers by XLE America
Cover Photos by Lisa Sinclair

ISBN-13: 978-0615835938

ISBN-10: 0615835937

First Edition: August 2013

DEDICATION

First and foremost, I would like to dedicate this book to the most important and special man in my life; my father Samahd Lewis. Although he spent most of my childhood and upbringing incarcerated, he made sure my grandmother and family raised me into the man I am today.

I also want to thank the people that helped me along the way through all my ups and downs. I wrote this book while incarcerated; I was able to sit back, think, and view life differently. I am extremely grateful and thankful God placed so many good, positive, and uplifting people in my life. If it wasn't for them, sad to say, but I'm sure I'll probably be incarcerated again.

Another thank you goes to all the Hommies in the hood, I definitely have to say thank you, because without you all and those slick ways I would not be me. I'm glad you all keep me on my toes.

Of course I had to save the best for last; my wife. I would like to thank the love of my life Latesha Hicks; she's my number one fan, and a team of her own. Throughout the years of me being incarcerated, she never once turned her back on me, and still managed to hold down our household, and raise my three beautiful daughters; she has been the motor behind my drive and I am beyond thankful.

CONTENTS

THE CITY

1
THE MEETING
OF
TWO

"Yo!" Samahd shouted getting the attention of his homeboy. "You see ol' girl right there? Good God Almighty, she a fool! Man, look how her ass move every time she walks."

"She outta ya league, Cuz."

"Nah, Fam, she ain't. As a matter of fact, watch this." Samahd ran across the street to catch the stallion walking down Bergen Street.

"What's good, baby? How you doin' today?"

"Excuse me," she began. "You're blocking my path, and I have somewhere I need to be."

"Just hold up for one second."

"You're a persistent dude, aren't you?"

"You could say that," Samahd chuckled. "My name is Samahd. What's your name?"

With an aggravated tone, she replied, "My name is Michelle."

"Okay, Michelle. You don't have to be so mean. I'm just tryna meet a new friend. I understand you're on your way somewhere. Could I at least get a contact number from you and we can continue this later?"

Against her better judgment, Michelle gave Samahd her number. *There's something about this dude I like, but I can't put my finger on it,* she thought to herself. *I just hope my boyfriend don't ride by and see me.* She broke her train of thought as she looked across the street to see a guy standing there staring at her as if he knew her. "Umm . . . Whose dude over there breakin' his neck to see what's going on over here?"

"That's just my man, BJ. Don't worry about him; he's cool. He's just over there hatin' on ya boy."

"Well, okay. I've got to get going. I forgot all about going to see my brother messing with yo' cute self," Michelle said as she gave Samahd a smile.

Samahd made his way back across the street to rejoin BJ.

"I told you I could get ol' girl with no problems. She seen you drooling outta the mouth while the kid was over there doing his thing."

Fiends came from every angle as Samahd and BJ stood on the block bangin' Al Green out of the speaker box of Samahd's brand-new '78 Cadillac Coupe deVille.

"What's good for tonight?" BJ asked as he split a Dutch Master. "I ain't tryna be on the block after ten."

"Fall back, my G. As soon as I finish these last two or three bundles, I'm gone. Besides, I need to call li'l baby girl before the night is out."

"What you mean, Fam? Don't start that BS chasin' no broad. It's Thursday night, and I know Branch Brook Park is jumping."

"Maybe you're right. I should give her at least a day or two before I call so she doesn't think I'm chasin' a broad. Ya dig?"

"Yeah, I dig. Nigga, you over there lookin' sick right now."

"Man, shut up 'cause it's about time you stop stashin' so much and grab you some wheels yo damn self."

"Oh, it's like that, huh? You got all the sense, Pimp Daddy Samahd."

"Come on, Nigga. It ain't even like that. You know it's Bergen until we fall."

"That's what's up."

"Now let's go get dressed for the skatin' rink."

Around 12'o clock that night, Samahd and BJ headed to the party. When they got there it was jumping. BJ notified Samahd that he was on a mission due to all of the broads scattered all about. As Samahd made his way around the skating rink, he played the crowd with so many women around. Branch Brook Park was on the north side of town. With Samahd and BJ being from the south side, they didn't know too many people. Despite that, he moved with persistence through the crowd as if he knew everyone in the building.

Just as Samahd passed through the arcade room, he happened to see a familiar face. Standing beside the lockers talking to another girl was Michelle. Samahd's heart skipped a beat as he noticed how beautiful she was. He tried to play it casual and walked over to Michelle as smooth as possible.

"What's good, baby?" Samahd greeted as he approached. "What you doing in here?"

"Nothing," she smiled. "My sister drug me out here. This isn't really my scene."

"I was getting ready to say. I knew I ain't never seen you out here before."

"I take it you've been here enough times by the way you moved around the room."

"So you were checkin' me out."

"Something like that."

"I was just tryna enjoy myself. You know . . . watch my surroundings. I gotta keep my eyes on these north Newark niggas."

"Boy, you silly," Michelle giggled. "How come you didn't call me today after you practically begged me for my number?"

Samahd smiled and said, "Girl, ain't nobody beg you. I just had to push a little harder given the circumstances that you didn't care for too much conversation."

"Yet you still talked me out of my number and didn't even use it."

"Anyway, we're here now. Where you going after you and your sister leave here?"

"Probably home. Why? What do you have planned for tonight?"

"Don't know. Most likely a little breakfast and some sleep. I've been out all day since I saw you this afternoon on Bergen."

"Uh-huh . . . you been out chasing those little girls running up and down Bergen Street."

"Nah, I don't do that too often. It's just that when I see someone as beautiful as yourself, I go out of my way to make myself noticeable. Ya dig?" Michelle laughed.

"Do you have any other conversation besides running game on me?" At that statement, Samahd couldn't help but grin.

"I'm for real. I saw then, and I see now something I like. Why you think I'm breakin' my neck every time I see you. That brings another question to my mind. What were you doing walkin' across Bergen Street all by yourself?"

"I told you. I was on my way to see my brother . . . which you made me late for."

"My bad, baby. Let me make it up to you by taking you to breakfast after this is over. I could go for some fish and grits."

"That sounds harmless. Let me go tell my sister, Donna, we're going to breakfast from here."

"Cool. I'll go tell my man BJ to get ready to go."

"What time is it?"

Looking at his watch, he replied, "It's 2:30."

"Okay. Let me go find Donna before she gets lost."

Michelle and Samahd went their separate ways. After about 20 minutes of searching through the large crowd, he found BJ at the skate counter talking to a broad.

"Yo, BJ!" he called as he motioned for him to come over. "What's good, Cuz? You all right?"

"I'm good . . . just over here talkin' to a new friend of mine." BJ turned toward the female and called to her. "Lisa! Come here for a minute." The young lady walked over to the two guys. "Samahd, this is Lisa. Lisa, this is Samahd."

"How you doing, Samahd?" Lisa greeted as she looked down and noticed he had on the same Gators BJ had on in a different color to match his outfit. "I like your shoes."

"Thanks, Ma," Samahd replied brushing Lisa off. "If you would excuse me for a minute,

12

I need to holla at my man for a sec."

"No problem." Lisa walked back toward the skate counter as BJ watched her every move.

"Bruh!"

"My bad, Cuz. What's good?"

"Let's bounce. I got a mission for us to go on. On top of that, I got a surprise for you."

"I'm listening."

"Remember baby girl I met on Bergen earlier this afternoon?"

"Yeah, I remember. You said you was gonna call her tomorrow or something."

"Now I don't have to. She's here."

"Word? I didn't see her. I bet she lookin' real good tonight."

"She is, but wait until you see her sister."

"What!" BJ shouted. "She got a sister? Stop playin'. Why didn't you tell me this before? I woulda been told you to call."

"Come on so we can go find 'em. I set it up for us all to go to breakfast at IHOP on Route 22."

"Boy, you a fool! I guess you got everything mapped out. Gimme a minute to get Lisa's number so I can get at her later."

Samahd and BJ found Michelle and Donna

sitting at the front door waiting on them to leave. As BJ got closer to Donna, he couldn't help but stare at how beautiful she was. He was amazed at how her hair went down her back into a perfect ponytail. He thought to himself, *Man, Samahd got me in a whole 'nother league.* They finally made it to the girls from across the room as Samahd introduced Donna and BJ. Donna looked him up and down as she was also impressed with what she saw.

"Come on," Michelle began interrupting Donna and BJ's epic gaze. "Let's go. I'm getting hungry, plus I'm trying to leave before the party lets out and the parking lot gets too crowded for us to get out."

Samahd agreed as the four of them made their way through the front door. As they got outside, he suggested that Michelle ride with him and BJ with Donna. They all agreed. A look of surprise spread across Michelle's face when she saw Samahd's car.

"Excuse me, Mr. Man. Whose car do you have?"

"This is just a little something I picked up. As a matter of fact, this is one of my favorites."

"Stop frontin'," Michelle laughed. "You're acting like this is your car and you have more than one."

Samahd laughed and opened the door for Michelle as he thought to himself, *Girl, if you only knew how we do it on the south side.*

As they pulled off of Hwy 22, Samahd thought to himself as he looked over at Michelle who fell asleep, *Man, this girl is bad. I could get used to being around her little thick self.* He pulled into the parking lot and found two open spaces.

"Michelle," he called. "Wake up, Sleeping Beauty."

"Wow, I didn't realize I fell asleep."

"You did, and you slobbed all on your seat right there."

"Oh my God, Samahd!" Michelle gasped and wiped her mouth. "Why did you say that? Now I'm embarrassed."

"It's okay, baby. I'm glad you're becoming comfortable around me. Being yourself is what I'd like best."

"Come on and stop talking so we can get something to eat before it gets too crowded in here."

Donna pulled into the spot right beside Samahd and Michelle. The two newfound friends were smiling when they got out. Samahd looked over and noticed the new Jaguar and realized that the girls weren't doing too bad either. He swung his arm around

Michelle and followed BJ and Donna into
IHOP. The four sat at a booth and had a great
time as they talked and ate.

"Michelle," Samahd began as he took a
sip of his orange juice, "what y'all trying to do
from here?"

"I don't know. Why? Do you have
something in mind?"

"I was thinking we could ride to New
York or something like that."

"I don't know where y'all going, but me
and BJ already have plans," Donna interrupted.

"So what's good, Michelle?"

"I'm a little sleepy, but I'd rather stay
with you. For some reason I just have a safe
vibe with you."

"That's what's up."

"Do you have somewhere in mind you'd
like to go?"

"No, but I know there's hotels on this
highway somewhere." Once again Donna
interrupted.

"I saw a hotel on the way here coming
through Hillside so it wouldn't be that far."

"That's what it is then. Let's bounce from
this joint."

2

Big News

Kareem Hicks

Samahd sat on the block in the cool AC of his car daydreaming while "For the Love of Money" slid out of his speaker at a low volume. He was thinking of his new baby and how good a time he had with her last month at the hotel. Since then, she'd spent almost every weekend with him, but she hadn't called him in about three days. Samahd was broken out of his daydream by a dope fiend knocking on his window. He opened the door and stepped out of his car for the first time that day. He'd been sitting on the block at the top of the hill watching the flow of money.

"What's good, G Boss?" Samahd greeted. "What's the word on the streets for the day, Cuz?"

"Everything is copasetic, cool, ya know."

"Okay, so why you knockin' at my window?"

"I was just tryna see if you could give ya boy a bundle for 65 right quick."

"Come on, G Boss. It's too early in the morning for this bullshit."

"I know, man. I just got a little lick over on Lehigh and the Backstreet waitin' on me."

"Why didn't you ask BJ? I just saw him not too long ago so I know he on the block somewhere."

"Come on, Samahd. You know he ain't

18

takin' no less than 80. Hell, that'll only leave me 20, and I can't hustle off of that. I would have to make another lick."

"All right!" Samahd started to get agitated. "Meet me at Ms. Ruth's house in five minutes."

"Man, damn, Samahd. Don't go in there and stay all long. You know how she gets around you."

"Anyway. I got you, man. Just come behind me in five minutes." Samahd pulled out his keys and walked in the house.

"Hey, Ruth," he greeted as he walked in. "How you doin', baby?"

"I'm good, but you know BJ been running back and forth all day. That boy should at least have about a hundred right now because this morning was crazy."

"Yeah, I see. It was like 250 bricks (5 bundles of heroin is a brick) in here, and it looks like about maybe 50. It's cool, though. I'm about to get right. Where is BJ anyway? Have you happened to see him in the last 30 minutes?"

"No, baby. I haven't seen him in about an hour."

"Okay. I'm getting ready to go outside and find him. I'll talk to you later, okay?"

"Well, when are you going to take care of

me?"

"I'll make sure I see you before the end of the day. Okay, baby?"

"Yes, Daddy. Just make sure you take care of an old woman."

Samahd walked out the door and found G Boss sitting on the step.

"Come on, Samahd," G Boss complained. "I been out here for 15 minutes waitin' on yo' slick ass. What was you in there doing?"

"Nigga, shut up and take this bundle."

G Boss tried to grab the bundle from him, but Samahd said, "Hold up. Money first."

"Here. Now give me my bundle." G Boss took the bundle from Samahd.

"Hey, man, where BJ at? You seen him today?"

"I just saw him walkin' across the Backstreet with some broad. If you hurry up you can catch him on Renner and the Backstreet."

"That's what's good, Cuz. I'll see you later on tonight at the 4 Leaf." Samahd jumped in the car and drove down the Backstreet the wrong way. He caught BJ about four blocks down.

"What's good, Fam?" Samahd greeted as he pulled up beside BJ and a female.

"You, Fam."

"Where you been all day?"

"I had to run a few errands for Mommy so she wouldn't start trippin'."

"I just came from Ruth's house and saw the stash. You good?"

While making a gesture toward his pockets and smiling, he said, "Of course I'm straight."

Samahd looked at the girl that was with BJ and noticed it was Donna. His heart skipped a beat. "Gimme a second so I can pull over and talk to you. The last thing I need is for Jake to pull up while I'm facing the wrong way on this one-way." He pulled over on Renner Avenue and jumped out, leaving the car running.

"Hey, Donna. What's good with your sister, Michelle? I haven't seen her in a couple of days."

"Umm," Donna hesitated. "I really don't know, Samahd. I guess she's been in the house chillin'."

"Come on, Donna. I know you know something. You live in the house with her."

"I don't know if I should be getting into y'all situation, Samahd."

"Look here, Donna. I'll make it worth your while. If you tell me what's really going on, I'll give you a grand ($1,000) for any information."

"Let me see the money in my hand first and I might just remember something about little sis."

Samahd placed the roll of money in Donna's hand in exchange for the information. "Okay, all I can tell you is that she has been in the house throwing up for the past couple of days. Now you draw up the conclusion from there."

"That's cool, Donna. You don't have to say anymore. Is your moms home or do you think I could stop by to see her for a few?"

"I don't know. She should be gone for a few hours so go ahead. If the Impala is gone, then my mom is gone. You should see the Jaguar in the driveway."

Michelle was at home losing her mind because of the dilemma she was in. She picked up the phone to call her boyfriend, Red, to explain to him how she's gotten pregnant.

"Red," she began, "I need to talk to you about something important, and you have been dodging me."

"No, I haven't. I been busy lately."

"Well, I've been sick lately, plus my period hasn't come yet."

"What do you mean, Michelle? How long have you felt sick?"

"Maybe about a week, but, Red, I have been trying to tell you."

"Michelle, what do you mean you been trying to tell me? You got a brand-new Jag that I bought you. You could have sat on my block and waited for me for something that important. Basically, what you're saying is you're pregnant."

"Yes, Red, I'm pregnant."

"Well, I don't care. It ain't mine, so do what you gotta do to fix the problem. Bye!"

Red slammed the phone down as he broke Michelle's heart. She sat crying, then heard the doorbell ring. She looked up wondering who it could be. Maybe Donna lost her key. She got up and walked to the door and slung it open. Michelle was surprised to see who was on the other side. Samahd saw the tears streaming down her face.

"What's wrong, baby?" Samahd attempted to console her. "Why are you crying so bad? It seems like somebody's done something to you."

Michelle began to cry even harder as she looked into Samahd's eyes. She knew it was time to explain to her new love what was going on.

"Samahd," she began as she gathered herself, "I have something to explain to you, but I don't want you to get upset."

"Okay, but can I at least come inside?"

"I'm sorry. Where are my manners? Come in. My mother won't be home until around 2 in the morning. She went to a fashion show."

"That's cool. So what's up, Michelle? Why are you crying so much?"

"Well," Michelle paused, took a deep breath, then exhaled. "Before I fell in love with you or before I met you, I had a boyfriend."

"So what . . . Is he bothering you or something like that? Because I can deal with the situation with no problem."

"It's not that he's bothering me, but I'm just going to come out and say it."

"Say what, Michelle?"

"Samahd . . . I'm pregnant."

"Okay, so what's the problem? I like kids."

"No, Samahd. I'm *three* months pregnant."

"Oh, I see what you're getting at. What does your ex-boyfriend have to say about you being pregnant?"

"He wants me to get rid of it, but my mother doesn't believe in abortions."

"Don't worry, baby. What's dude's name anyway?"

"They call him Red. He's from off of South Orange Avenue."

"Okay. I'll take care of it myself. You don't have to worry about this anymore. I promise you, Michelle. This will be my child, and no one will ever know otherwise."

Samahd started to kiss Michelle seductively across her chest and down her legs. She pulled him close to her, led him into her bedroom, and fell back on the neatly made queen-sized bed. Samahd hovered over her and continued to kiss his way from her lips to her clit. As he finally made his way down her caramel-toned body and stuck his tongue in her sex box, she started to shiver.

When Samahd first came to the door, she was wearing nothing but a T-shirt and panties, but now she was totally naked. Samahd worked his way out of his pants while he continued to caress Michelle's love box. She was at the closest point of climax when Samahd suddenly stopped and smoothly slid his ten-inch erection inside of her. Michelle thought to herself as she was in full-blown ecstasy, *I am so in love with this man.* At the close of that thought she reached the best orgasm she's ever felt.

Around 12:30 that night, Samahd left

Michelle's house with murder on his mind. He couldn't fathom the thought of how someone could treat the one he'd grown to love like that. Could Red really be that full of himself to treat Michelle that way? It didn't matter because Samahd was going to use all the muscle and power he had to find Red.

3
THE MUSCLE

Samahd called a meeting for all the heroin kings of each side. With there being only four, all under Abdule, it was easy to do. Everyone met at the Robert Treat Motel in downtown Newark. Samahd was the first to make it to the conference to set up for his meeting. Abdule Prey was the next to walk in the room. Not trailing far behind was Rashon Cooper, then Derrick Williams (D Roc). Last, but not least, was C T Hake. Once everyone got to the meeting, Samahd immediately began to talk.

"We have rules and regulations that we must go by in order to keep the peace," Samahd began. "All of our wives or main broads are off-limits. So, therefore, I have come to bring my woman and problem to this board. My girl's name is Michelle, and I'm trying to find this dude who has supposedly purposely disrespected her. D Roc, dude is from your side of town. The streets told me that he is from the S. Orange Avenue area. Do you know who this young up-and-coming hustler is?"

"Do you at least have the name of this little young blood?" D Roc asked.

"Yeah, his name is Red."

"Okay, now I know who you're talking about. He's one of my generals on that block."

"Well, I need to get at this kid as soon as

possible."

"Listen, man, don't hurt young blood. You can see him tomorrow around two, and I'll even meet you out there."

"That's cool, Fam. I will be there at 2 P.M. sharp."

Samahd pulled up on S. Orange Avenue and Bergen Street at about 1:20 in the afternoon. As he made the right onto S. Orange Avenue, he saw some dudes working out of the New Community Projects. He was sure that one of them was Red, Michelle's ex. He instructed his boys to pull into the parking lot as they waited for D Roc to show up. Samahd and BJ sat in the front seat of the first car watching the drug traffic as it moved rapidly in midafternoon. BJ thought to himself about how much money these dudes had to be making. He had plenty of blocks himself, but none boomed like this one in the middle of the day. While BJ was in the middle of his thought, D Roc pulled up on the side of the car. BJ rolled the window down.

"What's good, D Roc?" BJ greeted. "How you doing today, big homey?"

"Ah, man, I'm coolin' . . . Just floatin' in the breeze. Get ready to pull over and I'll get

Red so we can talk about this little situation." D Roc pulled into the New Community parking lot while Samahd stayed across the street and watched him.

D Roc got out of the car and walked to the crowd of young gunners talking to one another. "Yo, what's good, Young Bloods? What's poppin' for the day?"

Red walked out of the crowd and gave his big dog some love. "What brings you all the way outside this early in the day? You usually wouldn't show your face until seven o'clock, so what's good?"

"Nothing serious, Blood. I just need you to walk with me for a second to handle something."

"Okay . . . Where we walking to?"

"Right over here to the front parking lot to talk to my man."

Samahd looked and noticed a light-complexioned dude walking toward his car with D Roc. He stepped out as contrast to the T with the newest linen suit out. Red looked him up and down wondering what this was all about. Samahd started the conversation.

"How you, Little Cuz?"

Immediately, Red took offense at Samahd calling him cuz and tried to straighten him.

"Hold up, Blood. Ain't no cuz shit poppin off around here."

Samahd looked at the arrogant little prick before him and smiled. D Roc sensed the vibe Samahd had received and told him to have patience with the youngin'.

"He hasn't learned about much respect in business yet," D Roc explained.

"I understand D, but back to you, Red," Samahd replied in a sarcastic tone. "I'm here for a purpose that I would like to talk to you about."

BJ jumped out of the car and made way to the circle seeing the vibe in them.

"You used to talk to a female that I know. What I would like is for you not to bother her anymore."

"So who might that be you're concerned about?"

"Her name is Michelle. She's a woman that has become very dear to my heart."

"She's a nobody. I got the broad pregnant and told her she needed to handle it because I'm too young to have kids."

"Look here, Li'l Nigga," Samahd said grabbing him by his collar and throwing his .357 in his face. "If you ever do as much as come close to her again, I'll push yo' whole shit back myself."

D Roc stepped in between them as BJ drew his Mac 11 from the waistline.

"Now, please, fellas," BJ said to D Roc and Red. "We don't want this to get ugly."

D Roc called on Samahd to remain calm. "We have too much to lose over him." Red looked at D Roc in amazement.

"This man in front of you is one of the Four Kings, which means he is untouchable. So we must respect his wishes as he asked."

"Okay, Blood. Just let me go and we're cool."

"Samahd, listen," D Roc began. "I want to apologize for young blood getting out of order. I have to spend a little more time with them. Then I could teach them the way things go when you're dealing with big business."

"Yeah," Samahd replied tucking his gun back in his waist. "You do that so I don't have to teach that little mutt a lesson in manners. I'm gone, D. I'll get with you later. Come on, BJ. Let's ride so we can get back to the south side."

"Yeah, let's do that because my finger's really starting to itch."

As Samahd and BJ got back in the car and drove down the street, Samahd showed how angry he was.

"I'm telling you, BJ, we gon' catch this little nigga somewhere and push his whole face back!"

"Okay, Cuz. Just calm down before you run into something or somebody on the way back. I already knew when he talked to you like that on some gang shit that he was going to have to go." BJ knew that the Four Kings made a peace treaty with gangs so that everyone could keep the blocks pumping. "Now since Red has come at my big homie, Samahd, on some gang trash, I know he's hot," BJ said joking with the little homies in the backseat.

"Man, shut up and stop playin' so much," Samahd said to BJ.

"Okay, man, fall back and take it easy."

"No. Now when we get back to the block, I got a surprise for you."

"What's that, man? The last time you had a surprise for me, I 'bout fell in love."

"Well, guess what? If you think you fell in love with some pussy, you gon' fall head over heels over this."

When Samahd and BJ got back to Bergen Street, they pulled on Mapes and parked their cars. As they got out, Samahd called BJ and told him to walk with him to Ruth's house, which was on Mapes as well.

"Yo, watch this when we get in here and don't be all loud and wake Ruth because she will be trying to keep me in the house to give her some dick. Bad enough I haven't hit her in at least a week or two," Samahd and BJ broke out laughing as they walked up the steps.

4

THE BEGINNING

OF AN

END

Michelle was in the house getting dressed to go to the doctor for a 3:30 appointment when she heard her door coming off the hinges. "Who in the hell is banging on my mom's door like that?"

She finished getting dressed as she walked to the door. *Boom! Boom! Boom!* was all she heard as she got closer to the door. She looked through the peephole to see who it was. Red was screaming so loud she could hear him like he was standing in the room with her. Michelle wondered if she should open the door while Red was looking and acting mad. Then she remembered that Samahd had told her they had no worries. She slung the door open throwing on the best game face she could muster.

"Boy!" Michelle barked. "Why in the hell are you banging on my mama's door like that?"

Red pushed past the door and immediately smacked Michelle in the face, sending her hard to the floor. Michelle grabbed her face and jumped up. "What's wrong with you putting your hands on me like that?"

"So now you playing stupid, sending your so-called new boyfriend to my block telling me not to see or touch you anymore. To make shit worse, he had my OG on his side and embarrassed me in front my homies like I'm some little street punk."

"I didn't know, Red. I have no idea what's going on in the streets. I just told him what you told me and how I felt on the situation."

"Okay . . . How do you feel about the matter?"

"For one, I'm not getting rid of my baby, and for two, I don't need you."

Out of nowhere, Red punched Michelle in the stomach.

"Well, you had better know something, bitch!" Red turned around and stormed out of the door. Michelle sat there holding her stomach crying in astonishment from what had just happened to her. She crawled to the phone that was sitting by the couch. She called Samahd over at Ruth's house. Ruth picked up the phone on the third ring.

"Hello, may I know who's calling, please?"

"Hi, this is Michelle. Can I speak to Samahd, please?"

"Sure you can, young lady. Give me one second."

"Okay, ma'am. Thank you so much."

"Are you okay, young lady?" Ruth asked

noticing the tone of her voice. "You sound troubled."

"I'm just a little under the weather is all. Thank you for asking."

"Okay, give me one second to go find him."

Ruth walked to the front door to see if she could find Samahd anywhere. As soon as she opened the door, Samahd and BJ were walking up the steps laughing. "Oh hell, what are you two boys up to?"

"Nothing, Ruth. Why what's up with you? Where you going?"

"Nowhere . . . I was coming to get you."

"For what? Are you okay?"

"I'm fine, but some young girl named Michelle is on the phone, and for some strange reason she's crying."

"What! Why is she crying? Did she say?"

"No, Samahd. She's still on the phone."

"Okay. BJ and I have something to show you anyway." Samahd ran in the house and picked up the phone.

"Hello. What's up, baby? Why did you call crying?"

"Samahd, I have something to tell you, and I don't want you to be upset."

"What's up, baby? You can tell me anything; it's okay."

"Well, for some reason, Red came over here today and banged on my door until I opened it. Then he rushed the door, smacked me on the face, and punched me in my stomach."

"Are you kidding me, Michelle?"

"Samahd, I wouldn't have called you crying my heart out telling you this if it wasn't true. On top of that, I have a doctor's appointment today at 3:30."

"Make sure you go and tell me what happens when you get back. I'll take care of everything else myself; don't even worry."

Michelle hung up the phone relieved at what Samahd told her. She went into the bathroom and hurried to finish getting dressed.

Samahd was furious at what Michelle had just told him. He slammed the phone down so hard that it broke into pieces. Ruth just looked at him and didn't say a word because she knew firsthand how deadly Samahd could be when he was that angry. She thought to herself about the time Samahd shot a man dead in the face after he made a mistake and killed her son Jimmy in a car wreck. Samahd broke Ruth's train of thought as he yelled for BJ to come in the house.

"What's good?" BJ asked as he walked in. "What's the word with Michelle?"

"This li'l nigga done lost his motherfuckin' mind!" Samahd roared. "He went over to Michelle's, smacked her and punched her in the stomach to hurt my baby."

"What the hell you mean your baby? Why didn't you tell me what was up, Cuz? I knew she was sick when Donna said something, but I never paid it any more attention after that. So what we gonna do about ol' boy?"

"He just helped my plan more than he knows. That's also part of your surprise. I got something for you and me." Samahd turned to Ruth. "Do me a favor, Ruth. Grab that box with those new toys in it."

"Gimme a second," Ruth replied. "Hell, I need a shot with all this going on."

BJ smiled as he knew what Samahd was talking about when he said go get the new toys. He loved guns almost as much as he loved pussy. That's why Samahd kept him as his right hand. He knew BJ was always ready for gunplay.

Ruth came out of the back room, which used to be her son's room, with two long boxes.

"What the hell are those?" BJ asked.

"Those are the newest Mossbergs with all the modifications you could want. Straight killing machines . . . If you know what I mean."

"So let me see what we got, Cuz."

"Hand me the boxes please, Ruth."

"Here you go, Samahd, but before I give these to you, promise me something."

"What is it, Ruth?"

"I want you to be as careful as you can. Make sure you don't get reckless and make any mistakes."

"I will. Now can I please talk to BJ? Alone."

Ruth walked out of the room as Samahd opened the boxes and pulled out two pistol grip, eight-shot pumps. They were sawed off at the tip for extra spray action. BJ's eyes got so big they almost popped out of his head.

"Yo, Cuz! Where the hell did you get these from?"

"Don't worry about all that. Just let me know how you like 'em."

"Like 'em? I *love* 'em. These are the hardest toys I've seen. I'm gettin' ready to do some pure damage with these, for real."

"Just be easy, Cuz. We got plans to follow through with tonight."

"So what's the plan?"

Samahd and BJ sat down and devised a plan for them to touch Red as soon as possible. "Let's just go spray the whole block up wit' these pretty thangs. Ain't no way we could miss with all this spray action."

"Yeah, but neither of us wants to get shot or go to jail for slippin', so that won't work."

"So what do you have in mind?"

"Well, first of all, we have to do something to surprise him. Then we have to get him by himself."

"You know what?"

"What, man? Stop playin'. I got it. Call your girl, Gena, the broad that just started snortin'. She bad as hell, and she can serve the purpose for my plan."

"I'm on it right now."

5
THE PLAN

Michelle made it to her doctor's appointment around 3:10 that afternoon. She went into the office and checked in. After about 10 minutes, a nurse came out and called Michelle's name. She stood up and walked through the door.

"Hello, Doctor Simms," Michelle greeted her as she walked into the examination room.

"How are you today, Ms. Hicks?"

"I'm fine, or at least I hope I'm fine, if you know what I mean."

"Of course, I do. Now get up on the table so I can go ahead and check you out, young lady."

Michelle lay back on the table hoping her baby was okay. Dr. Simms began her examination, and in no time it was over. "Everything is fine with you and the baby. You are three and a half months, and the baby is getting big very quickly."

"Thank you, Dr. Simms. I am so thankful to have you as my doctor."

"Well, see me this time every month until you are about a month away from your due date."

"Okay, I'll do that. Is there any other advice you can give me or anything else I need to know?"

"Actually, there is. Make sure you don't

do any drinking or engage in stressful activities."

"Yes, ma'am. I will do just that."

Samahd, BJ, Gena, and one of her girls met on Bergen around 8:30 that night. As the two girls pulled up, Samahd thought to himself, *I hope they do right. I swear!*

"Come on, BJ. It's time to put this plan to work."

Samahd and BJ jumped in the backseat of the car the two females were in.

"I need you to do me a favor, Gena."

"Yes, baby," she replied in a seductive tone. "Anything for you, Samahd." Gena had heard so much about Samahd that she was dying to meet him. She knew what it was worth to do anything for him. Gena thought to herself, *All I have to do is whatever he asks me to do and I will surely be up under his wing.*

Samahd broke her train of thought. "Gena, I need you to drive down Bergen to New Community."

"Which parking lot you want me to go in?"

"The second one toward the back. Take this money. It's $300. All I want you to do is go get a bundle first and come back."

"Okay, baby. Let me do this. I got you."

Gena pulled up in New Community about 20 minutes later. She hopped out of the car and walked over to Red and his crew. Samahd and BJ sat in the back of Gena's brand-new Buick Regal Limited Edition. They watched the whole thing as Gena went and got the bundle while Red pushed up on her trying to get some play. Gena played her part to a tee as she told him she would be right back as soon as she finished the bundle. She walked back to the car with the best walk she could possibly do. Red was so turned on by her.

"Yo, Ma!" he yelled across the lot. "Hurry up and finish that. The next one's on me!"

"Okay, baby!" she hollered back. "Let me get right. I'm just going to be over here!" That's all Samahd needed to hear. His plan was going so good, he couldn't believe it himself. When Gena got back to the car she asked, "Was that good enough for you, baby?"

"That was cool. Now pull up to the parking lot at the top so we can finish this up."

"You got it. Is there anything else you need for me to do?"

"Of course. Hurry up and do that free bundle, then walk back down there like you did before. This time, bring the dude you were talking to back to the car with you."

Gena hurried up with her dope, then got back out of the car. She snorted five bags and gave the other five to her girl in the front seat. Before Gena could make it down to Red, he saw her coming and started walking toward her.

"How did that new thing do for you, baby?" Red inquired as he got closer to her.

That cut-up shit, Gena thought to herself. *Samahd's is ten times better*. "It did me good, baby. Can I get another bundle because then I'll be great."

"I got you. Where you park at?"

"On the top so me and my girl could get right."

"So it's two of you to play with."

"Of course. Did you think I was the one for jokes?"

"You know I'm tryna see both of y'all, right?"

"Boy, don't be silly. Come on and I'll show you who's down."

"Well, then, let me see how real you are, Ma. What's your name, by the way?"

"I'm Gena, and you?"

"I'm Red."

"Let's go, Red."

As Samahd saw Gena and Red coming

back to the car, he told BJ to lock and load.

"All right, Cuz," Samahd began. "You get out and get behind the car. When you hear the door getting ready to open, jump out from behind and throw that thang to his head. I got the rest."

"That's what's up," BJ replied as he got out of the car.

Samahd lay down in the backseat as Gena and Red got closer to the car. As soon as Red got to the car he started to speak to Gena's girl.

"What's poppin'?" he greeted as he approached the car. "How you doin', gorgeous?"

"I'm fine. How you doin'?"

"I'm good."

"Shut up, Nigga!" BJ interrupted. "Put ya hands up and don't move."

On cue, Samahd came up from the backseat of the car throwing the pump in Red's face. "What the fuck did I tell you about Michelle?"

As Red began to stutter, BJ and Samahd pulled the trigger at the same time, severing Red's body parts, which flew in all directions. The damage from the sawed-off pumps was so extreme, BJ was surprised at the results.

"Damn, Cuz! These things is crazy! You

hear me? I need some more action."

"Let's go!" Samahd demanded pulling BJ in the car. "Go, Gena, and don't look back!"

"Yes, baby," Gena obliged as she sped off. "Just calm down."

Samahd finally finished the final part of his plan as they rode back to his side of town.

"Pull on Nye and Clinton Place so I can get something."

"Okay, baby. We'll be there in a few. Just relax while I turn the music up and finish my bags."

Samahd sat back and looked over at BJ. He noticed he was taking his gloves off and punched his leg. Samahd told BJ to keep his gloves on. BJ smiled, knowing what else Samahd had in mind for them.

"Pull over right there behind that Impala."

Gena pulled over still bouncing to the music. Samahd and BJ quickly put the pumps to the girls' heads and pulled. Then the two got out of the car. Samahd took one final look at the headless bodies.

While shaking his head, BJ said, "You need some help, Samahd. Those was some bad broads. We coulda used them again."

"Yeah, and we coulda went to jail for life, too. You choose which one was the best."

"You might be right. Just know that but know that Gena might've had the best pussy in Newark—even with her habit."

"If it's that good, then stick ya dick in her one last time."

BJ looked at Samahd, and the two of them busted into laughter as they walked to the stolen car they already had parked on Clinton. They jumped in and peeled out en route to the block.

Samahd and BJ stood on Mapes on the late night smoking.

"BJ," Samahd began as he passed him the joint, "I just want to thank you for holding me down tonight."

"You know I always got ya back, Fam."

"I know, but you showed me a true friend back there. For that, I have something in return. Now don't get big headed, but here you go." Samahd tossed him a set of keys.

"What's this?"

"It's yours. Come on so I can show you what you have." They walked to the top of the hill to Mapes Place and stood next to a brand-new Cadillac Fleetwood.

"Man, what the hell? Whose is this?"

"Just jump in and enjoy yourself. I got to

go to Michelle's house for the night. Her mom is gone for the weekend. I'll see you tomorrow . . . bright and early."

"*That's* what's up, Cuz. We got a day to make up for."

Samahd jumped in the car with BJ and told him to drop him off at his car.

Michelle sat in the house waiting on her man. She was more than happy to have someone to truly love her and her baby more than all. "I can't wait for my baby to get here so I can show him how important he is to me," she said to herself. At the close of her statement, she heard a knock at the door.

"One second!" Michelle called as she ran to the door. When she opened the door, Samahd was standing there with a dozen red roses.

"Roses for the lady," he smiled.

"Thank you, baby! They're beautiful. Come on in. You hungry?"

"Not really. I'm just ready to go to bed. I had a long day."

"Are you okay?"

"I'm good. I just have an early start to a long day tomorrow."

"OK, then, let's go to bed."

Samahd lay in the bed thinking about what all had taken place in the last few months. He was happy with his life and ready to move on.

The next morning, Samahd woke up and got ready to go outside. Michelle woke up when she felt Samahd stirring.

"Hey, baby," she greeted him as she stretched. "You getting ready to leave this early in the morning?"

"Yes, baby."

"Samahd, it's still dark outside."

"I know. This is what time I leave out every morning. You know the early bird gets the worm."

"I've heard that before, but I don't know how true it is."

"I'll show you how true it is by the time I come home." Samahd grabbed his gun from the nightstand and walked out the door.

6

NOT SO

INNOCENT

BJ sat on Mapes with G Boss at about 6:30 that morning.

"A, G Boss, go get me two bundles outta the alley for that broad right there. She said she's going to circle the block."

"All right, give me about 2 seconds, and I'll be right back. They in the Newport box by the trash, right?"

"Yeah, they should be."

BJ stayed with a lot of people in front of him chasing the Blue Magic they had.

Samahd saw all the people on the block and smiled. He knew he had one of the best blocks in Newark with the strongest heroin because he cut his dope the least of all the Four Kings.

BJ stepped in the middle of the street flagging down Samahd's car. Samahd looked up and saw BJ and stopped right by them.

"What's good, Fam?"

"Nothing, man, I'm coolin'."

"Guess what, though?"

"What's that, BJ?"

"It's been jumping out here this morning. I've been here about 45 minutes, and I done ran through about six bricks."

"No doubt. Let me park the car and I'll help you so we can get right today." Samahd pulled up the hill and hopped out of the car fresh as ever. He walked down Mapes to catch up with BJ and G Boss.

"What's up, G Boss?" Samahd said as he approached them.

"I can't call it. What's the word, Samahd? I like them ostrich thangs you got one right there. What's that, baby blue or something?"

"You know how I do," Samahd laughed. "BJ, what's going down today? It's Friday, and something's jumping off for sure."

"I heard they're having a pool party at Green Acres on Lyons Avenue around seven or something like that."

"You trying to go?" Samahd asked.

"Of course, you know I'm trying to go. I'm ready to bring the new whip out, you feel me?"

"Damn right. Now I can ride with you for a change."

"Oh no, my dude. You gotta drive your own car," BJ laughed.

"You for real?"

"Nah, man . . . I'm just jokin'."

"I was getting ready to get heated."

"Get mad so I can show you my new moves."

"I don't fight. I shoot." The two friends

laughed. "Let's go get something to eat."

"Listen here," G Boss interrupted. "I'ma stay out here while it's still moving fast."

"All right, G," BJ responded. "I got two more bricks right here. Hold these until I get back."

"These should be gone by the time you get back the way it's jumpin' out here."

Samahd stood up and waited for BJ to finish talking to G Boss so they could go eat. The two men walked down Bergen and into the 4 Leaf. The restaurant was crowded as usual. They found a seat in the back. After ordering two helpings of fish and grits and two coffees, the conversation began.

"I counted the bricks we had in Ruth's house," Samahd began as he moved his silverware to the side and propped his elbows on the table. "There were about 32 left."

"How many do you think we have left now?"

"I don't know how many are left now, but I know I took out 10 this morning. And I have two and some change left."

"Okay. I'm about to let Sadeek get 20 wholesale."

"Then we need to get right again."

"That's cool with me. I'll go get the last two joints and hold them."

"I might just let them go myself to get them last couple of dollars to burn at the pool party."

"You do that, then let me hold something."

"You know you can get it."

The food came as a breaking newscast caught Samahd's attention.

"This just in," the reporter began. *"Three bodies were found on two sides of town with the same MO. One man was found brutally slain in a New Community parking lot. The other two were found in a car on Clinton Place with both of their heads missing. The NPD has no leads and asks if anyone knows anything to come forward."*

"That's what I'm talkin' about," Samahd smiled.

"That was real clean, Fam."

"Yeah, it was a good plan, but it couldn't have went any better than what it did."

Michelle was sitting up watching the news when the same broadcast came through. She yelled at the top of her lungs.

"Donna! Come in here!"

"What you want, girl? Calling me like you crazy. I was eatin', and you made me drop my fork."

"Somebody just got killed in New Community and two people died on Clinton Place. The police said they're connected. I wonder who died in New Community. Will you go and find out?"

"Why do you want me to go and find out?"

"Because if Samahd found out that I went through there, he'd be pissed."

"Fine, I'll go after I get dressed. You got something for me?"

"Like what, Donna?"

"A bag of that Blue Magic."

"I got that put up. Samahd would kill me if he knew I was messin' wit' the nose candy."

"If you ask me, you better tell him before somebody else tells him."

"I just need to find a good time to tell him."

"Anyway, I have a bundle in my car."

"Bring me a bag for this morning before you leave."

"All right. Let me go and get dressed because it's already after nine."

"Okay . . . I'm going to lie down for a while."

Donna pulled into the New Community and saw what looked like a million candles in the top parking lot. She pulled into a space and got out to see what was going on. People were everywhere. She asked a young girl what happened and who died.

"Don't you watch the news?" the girl replied. "Red got killed last night."

"Oh my God! How did he die?"

"They say he was shot, but no one could tell with the way the body was tore in all types of pieces."

"Thank you. I have to go." Donna jumped in her car and sped off on her way back home to tell Michelle the news.

D Roc was sitting at a diner on Springfield Avenue when the waitress called him and told him he had a phone call. He knew it was important because only his generals could call him on the phone.

"What's the word, Blood?" D Roc answered. "Is everything good in the hood?"

"Nah, Big Dog. Somebody killed Red last night."

"Who?"

"I don't know, D Roc. All we know is he went to make a sell to some chick and never came back."

"So who is this and how did you get this number?"

"This is Taywan. I was Red's right-hand man. I'm from Prince Street, but I kept close to Red."

"What happened when he didn't come back?"

"We walked up top to see where he was, and we found him dead on the ground."

"This is what I want you to do. Call a meeting for your crew and I'll be there around five."

"I'm on it, Big Dog."

D Roc hung up the phone knowing that there was only one person that had the balls to pull off such a murder in Red's own hood. He thought about how upset Samahd was at Red just days before. No one else knew but him. Once he saw Samahd he would have some questions for him. *I know Samahd doesn't want a war*, he thought to himself. *How could he disrespect me like that?* He had to find him so they could talk. D Roc jumped in his brand-new red Z280 and took off like lightning.

Samahd, BJ, and a couple others stood on Mapes shooting the breeze. BJ was the only one with a couple of bundles to sell. Everyone else was waiting for Samahd and BJ to get right. Samahd looked up and saw Sadeek walking down Bergen from Lehigh.

"What's good?" Samahd greeted.

"You got something for me?" Sadeek asked.

"Yeah, come on." They walked off from the rest of the group. "What took you so long to come outside today?"

"I had this bad chick last night."

"In other words, you sayin' you had a long night."

"You could say that."

"Who was she? Do I know her?"

"Nah, she's one of my little man's sisters."

"No doubt. How many you tryna get?"

"How many you got?"

"I can let you get about 20."

"Let me get all 20. What's the number for 'em?"

"For you? Give me 3 a piece. That's $6,000."

"Here you go." Sadeek handed Samahd the money. "When can I get 'em?"

"Give me a minute to go in the house. I'll be right back." Samahd went in the house and came back out a few minutes later. As he walked out the door, BJ met him. "What's up, BJ?"

"Nothing. D Roc outside up Mapes a little. He wants to talk to you."

"All right. Tell 'em I'm on my way." Samahd handed Sadeek the packages, then went to meet D Roc up the street.

D Roc sat on Mapes waiting for Samahd to come out. He thought to himself, *Look how this young nigga got all these people out here runnin' around like ants. Why are all his people turning fiends away? I know this little nigga ain't finish his 20 blocks before me.* Samahd broke his train of thought when he knocked on the window.

D Roc quickly opened the door trying not to show Samahd his hate.

"What's going on, Fam?" Samahd greeted as he jumped in the car.

"I'm coolin'. What's up with you?"

"Ah, man, I'm on the block kickin' it with the homies. Ya feel me?"

"Yeah, I can dig it."

"What the hell kinda wheels are these?"

"This that new Z280. You ain't ready for this thang right here. She move so fast you can barely see her in motion."

"I see you," Samahd laughed. "So what brings you to my side of town?"

"Damn, I almost forgot. Did you hear? My little blood got killed last night."

"Who you talkin' about, D?"

"My little dog, Red, that we talked to the other day."

"Nah, I didn't hear about that. How did he die?"

"He was shot so badly that they could barely identify the body. They had to use his dental work."

"Damn, Cuz. I didn't know. Do you have a clue because we can ride if you want."

"Not yet, but I will do my homework to find out who he was beefin' wit' and why."

"If you find somethin' out, let me know. I gotta go catch up with Abdule so I can get right."

"Are you kidding me, Samahd? You mean to tell me you finished all 20 blocks off that last move?"

"Yeah, man. I went through 'em like it was nothin'."

"You on a mission, I see."

"It's just supply and demand."

"All right, little homie. I'll check you later. I gotta get back to the other side to have a small meeting."

"I'll see you later on. Be easy, my G." Samahd jumped out of the car.

D Roc went down to the bottom of the hill, spun his car and shot back up the street—all in first gear with tires spinning. Samahd and BJ laughed as D Roc tried his best to show off.

"You see this nigga, BJ?"

"Yeah, I caught the drift. So, what was he so anxious to talk to you about?"

"Oh, you know what he was talkin' about, but I don't know," Samahd laughed once again. "Let's go find Abdule before it gets too late. You know he ain't tryna do nothing after 1 o'clock. If I can't get all the way right, I need to get 10 blocks before he gets low."

They rode to Meeker and Elizabeth Avenue to catch Abdule. Samahd pulled onto Meeker and saw Abdule sitting on his car. He jumped out and walked toward Ab while BJ walked into the store paying close attention to make sure Samahd was OK.

"What's the word for the day, Ab?"

"I got a good one for you today, Samahd."

"Oh yeah? What's that?"

"Keep your friends close and your enemies even closer."

"That's some good word right there."

"What brings you down here today?"

"I'm doin' bad."

"What do you mean, Samahd? You can't

do bad."

"Yes, I can."

"How is that?"

"Run outta dope too fast."

A huge smile spread across Abdule's face. "You mean to tell me you finished 20 bricks in two weeks?"

"To be honest with you, it took me a week and a half. It's only Friday."

"Boy, you gon' make the mayor give you the key to the city."

"You know what, Ab? I just might like that."

"Man, you crazy?"

"Believe me, Ab, I'm just tryna stay sane."

"So tell me, Little Cuz, what are you up to?"

"I'm tryna see if I can get 20 more, if that's all right with you."

"I can do that, but tell me one thing."

"What's that?"

"What's your secret for moving so fast?"

"If I tell you that, I wouldn't be useful to you now, would I?"

"You know what, Samahd? You got a point. Hell, I might have to make you my right hand."

"Now that would be nice."

"I might just have to think that one through. Here, take these keys."

"What's this for, Ab?"

"You see that old Camaro sitting up the hill?"

"You talkin' about the red one all the way up there?"

"Yeah . . . that one. You can keep it."

"Come on, man. What are you up to?"

"I don't know. I'm just in a giving mood today. Just make sure you give me the change. You feel me?"

"I can do that."

"All right . . . just take it and be careful. Oh yeah, and Samahd."

"What's up, Ab?"

"We have a little something to talk about. Do you feel where I'm coming from?"

"I think so. We'll talk later."

"Make sure you make time for your uncle Ab. You know the Kings' meeting is two weeks away."

"Yeah, I know."

"Just talk to me before then."

"All right, Ab . . . I'll see to it for sure."

Turning to BJ, he said, "Come on, BJ. Let's go. Just follow me."

"Where we going?"

"To Ruth's house. Stay close behind me."

"Let's ride."

7

TIME TO BLOW

Samahd pulled up to Ruth's house and parked the car. BJ pulled next to him sitting in the middle of the street.

"Samahd," BJ called from the window, "you straight or do you need my help?"

"I'm good. Where you gettin' ready to go?"

"I'm rollin' downtown to get something to wear for tonight."

"Come back as soon as you finish. We need to talk about these new thangs. It should be 10 or 20. Ab didn't say."

"If that's the case, I'll just keep your car so I can come right back."

Samahd looked back and forth before opening the trunk to the old Camaro. When it popped open, Samahd couldn't believe his eyes. He couldn't tell how many bricks were in there. He quickly closed the trunk, then ran in the house.

"Ruth!" he called as he walked through the door.

"Boy, what in the hell is wrong with you?"

"I need a garbage bag or something so I can grab all my clothes out of the car."

"Go in the kitchen and look under the

sink. There's a whole box down there. I just bought them today."

"Thanks, baby. I'll be back in a minute."

Samahd grabbed a bag and ran back out the door. He went to the car and opened the trunk to make sure he wasn't dreaming. As it was the first time, the trunk was full of bricks.

He opened the bag and began to fill it to the rim. When the last brick was in the bag, the final count was 43. "I'm going to crank up the whole city with this right here!" he said to himself as he closed the trunk and walked back into the house. Samahd couldn't fathom the amount of money he was going to make off the flip. He sat on the bed in amazement. He couldn't believe he had 43 bricks of pure heroin.

"Hey, Ruth," he called. "Come in here for a second." Ruth poked her head in the door. "Take this bag, put it in the back closet, and lock it until tomorrow morning. When you finish, come back in here. I got something for you."

Ruth got excited as she dragged the bag across the floor and stuffed it into the closet. She hurried back into the room where Samahd was lying on the bed.

"Come here, girl," he smiled. "Sit on the bed right here."

Ruth sat on the bed next to Samahd as he started to kiss her all over her neck, working his way to her stomach. He easily pulled her pants off as he caressed and kissed her thighs. Ruth began to moan as Samahd sexed her. He found her clit and rolled his tongue around and around just right. She grabbed his head and came in his mouth. Samahd quickly lifted his head up and smiled as he slid ten inches of manhood into Ruth's love box.

"Oh my God!" Ruth moaned in ecstasy. "Samahd, hold me!" As he did what he was instructed to do, Ruth began to come again. This time, it was all over his manhood. Samahd laughed to himself because he knew just what to do when it came to sexing Ruth out of her mind. He moved hard in and out of her love box until he reached his destination point. He pulled out and came all over Ruth's pussy.

"Damn, girl," Samahd exhaled. "You been practicin' for ya boy?"

"Maybe," Ruth replied with a sly grin. "Why? Are you getting used to it?"

"That's definitely something I could get used to."

BJ bounced to the music blaring out of the speakers of Samahd's car as he approached the block from downtown. *These new purple and yellow Gators are crazy!* he thought to himself. *I'm gonna shut the whole park down.*

G Boss waved him down when he saw Samahd's car cruising down Bergen.

BJ slowed down and pulled to the curb. "What's crackin' on the block?" he inquired.

"We got a problem."

"What's the problem?"

"Everybody tryna get that Blue Magic, but ain't nobody got none."

"Damn! Can't the dope man take a break every now and then and treat himself?"

"That's true, but now you're back. Where's my pack?"

"You got a comeback for everything, don't you?" BJ laughed. "All right, man, meet me on Mapes. Samahd should be outside somewhere." BJ took off down Bergen showing the power of the 'Lac. When he got to Mapes he pulled over, jumped out, and headed toward Ruth's house. He called for Samahd as he walked in the house.

"I'm in the back!" Samahd replied when he heard BJ's voice.

BJ walked into the room.

"You just gettin' back from downtown?"

"Yeah. It was packed down there, but, Cuz . . . they got the new shipment of Gators in."

"Word! What colors they got?"

"Any color you want. I scooped up the purple and yellow joints to match the linen suit I picked up."

"You tryna kill 'em, ain't you?"

"You know I gotta rep' for da hood. Speakin' of the hood, everybody sick. The only one that had dope was Sadeek, and now he's out."

"Well, I got a surprise for you."

"You and your damn surprises," BJ laughed. "What's up now? Ab hit you wit' about 10 or 20 bricks? That's a given, so let's get to work."

"You think you know everything, don't you? Follow me." Samahd led BJ to the closet where Ruth put the stash. When he opened the closet, pulled out the bag and opened it, BJ's eyes got as big as plates.

"Nigga! I ain't never seen this much dope in my life."

"The thing about it is that once we put the cut on it, the cut is all profit."

"This shit is crazy."

"Are you gonna help me move this shit, or are you gonna stand there droolin' on the bag?"

"You know this!"

"All right, but we gotta move fast before it starts to drop. You go get the girls, and I'll run get the cut so we can get this shit movin'." Samahd put the bag back in the closet, then he and BJ parted ways to get everything they needed.

Samahd was on his way back when he saw a line of bad females pouring into Ruth's house. He grabbed the bags and walked quickly into the house. When he entered, he didn't say a word at first. He stood and examined each female before he spoke.

"All right!" Samahd barked. "Everybody strip, go in the back, or go home!"

The girls were momentarily shaken up by the strength of his voice.

"Come on, ladies. You know what to do and exactly how I want it done. Face masks and everything else are right here." Samahd threw the bag to BJ and started toward the back room. He went into the closet and pulled out 10 bricks and laid them on the table—along with the rest of the tools. "Come here for a minute, BJ."

BJ walked over to his main man.

"Listen, we're going to do 10 at a time and see how fast they move."

"Got it."

"We can take over with this right here. I wanna show Abdule what we can do. I know if we can smash these in a timely manner, he'll have to put us second in command."

"Do you really think he will let us make it?"

"Of course, he will. He'll have no choice, BJ."

"The only one higher than Abdule is Frank. You do the math. If we move more than him, he would have to respect us."

"In that case, let's get it movin'."

BJ went into command mode. "All right, ladies, let's get it movin' . . . seven grams of cut to every ounce . . . nothing more and nothing less."

Samahd walked out of the room and into the kitchen where Ruth was.

"Ruth, I need you to stay on top of the girls. No slipups. Everything has got to be on point. You got me?"

"Boy, I heard you. Calm down."

"Talk shit," Samahd laughed, "without a doubt, I will not hesitate to punish that ass again."

"Maybe I need to be punished more often."

"Girl, cut it out. Me and BJ are gettin' ready to head out. We'll be back later tonight."

Samahd and BJ headed to his mother's
house, which was also on Mapes, to get dressed
for the party. Samahd walked into the house
with BJ right behind him carrying his clothes.

"Hey, Mom," Samahd greeted as he
kissed his mother on the cheek. "How are
you?"

"I'm fine, but I haven't seen you all
week."

"I know, Mom. I'm sorry. I've been over
at a new friend's house."

"So who is this new friend, Samahd?"

"Her name is Michelle, and she's special
to me."

"I understand that, son, but just be
careful."

"Yes, Mom. I'm trying my best. Now if
you'll excuse me, we have to get dressed to go
to a pool party."

"I guess that means I'll see you next
week."

"Come on, Mom, don't act like that."
Samahd reached into his pocket and pulled out
a wad of money. He peeled of twenty one
hundred dollar bills and handed them to his
mother. "Here, you go. Buy yourself something
pretty." Samahd loved his mother. Every week,
he made it a point to stop by and give her some
money. He always felt obligated to repay his

mother for the things she did for him and his brothers and sisters. His father, Billy, was hardly ever home because of his job. Billy was a fireman, so he was always at the firehouse. It didn't bother Samahd because he knew his dad had to take care of his family.

"Why you always gotta try to outdo me?" BJ laughed as Samahd pulled the tags off of his cream linen suit.

"Stop sweatin' me. You just get dressed so we can hit the road. It's already seven, and you know it's jumping out there. I'm tryna see what the females lookin' like."

"All right, man . . . gimme about 20 minutes and I'll be ready."

"Cool . . . I'm gonna call my baby and let her know when I'll be coming in tonight."

Michelle was walking in the house from running errands when the phone started ringing. She dropped her bags and ran to the phone. For some reason, she felt it was Samahd.

"Hello," Michelle answered.

"How's the lady in my life?"

"Hey, baby! What's up? I've missed you all day."

"I've missed you, too. That's why I called in the middle of the day."

"What have you been doing all day?"

"Nothing much . . . just runnin' around."

"Samahd, did you happen to catch the news this morning?"

"No . . . why do you ask?"

"Somebody killed Red last night. Rumor has it that he was shot so bad that his body was in pieces. They say that he's going to have to have a closed casket or maybe even be cremated."

"Oh man," Samahd replied suppressing his laughter behind the phone. "That sounds bad. Are you upset?"

"Not really. It just took me by surprise, you know?"

"I guess so. You need me to come by or something?"

"That's okay. I actually just walked in the house from buyin' some food for dinner."

"What you cookin'?"

"A little of this and a little of that. You just have to come in at a sensible hour to see."

"Well, if I'm not too busy, I will."

"Where you at now?"

"I'm over my mother's house on Mapes."

"Okay. If you need me, I'll be in the house for the rest of the night."

"I'll talk to you later."

"I love you, Samahd."

"Okay, bye." Samahd hung up the phone, lay back on the bed, and closed his eyes. *That girl really loves me.*

BJ broke his train of thought.

"Wake yo' ass up! We gotta go. You daydreamin' now?"

"Nah, man. Just thinkin' about Michelle."

"Everything straight?"

"Yeah, man . . . she's cooking dinner tonight, so I'm not stayin' out late."

"In that case, let's ride."

8

POOL PARTY

BJ and Samahd pulled up back-to-back in twin blue Cadillacs to the front entrance where everybody was. Samahd noticed the faces of people from the south side that he'd never seen before. He hopped out with his signature stroll. BJ was right behind him. Anyone who was anyone was in attendance. The two Newark hustlers slid through the crowd as they were hailed by everyone. When they got to the pool, they saw CT Hake and Abdule sitting by the pool taking shots.

"What's up, fellas?" Samahd greeted as he approached the two Kings.

"It's all about you, Young Blood," Abdule joked as he threw back a shot of liquor. "You in a league all by yo'self."

"Y'all niggas fall back."

"You know we just fuckin' with you, Samahd," CT interjected. "Standing there lookin' like a young Abdule."

"I'm tryin my damnedest. You know it's hard to keep up wit' Ab."

"Tell me about it. I been tryin' for the past six years to catch up with the Mack of the Year."

"Indeed," Samahd laughed. "By the way, Ab . . . thanks for the hooptie."

"You're welcome," Abdule smiled. "I thought you might need that li'l old car more than I did."

A group of girls approached the four men as BJ and Samahd were laughing at Abdule's words.

"What's so funny?" one of the young ladies asked.

"We were talking about how good you ladies look," CT answered before the others had a chance to respond. "The funny part was that I said that you would be the first one to talk. Now what's your name?"

"My name's Monique. What's yours, Smart Guy?"

"Who are these lovely ladies with you?"

"This is Shameka, Rasheeda, and that's Rochelle."

"What are you boys doing after the party?" Rasheeda inquired.

"I don't know," Abdule replied. "What did you have in mind?"

"Having some fun."

"What type of fun we talkin' about?" BJ smirked.

"The type of fun boys and girls have together," Rochelle answered winking at him.

"If that's the case, we all should get together and make our own party."

"The hell with all this talking," CT interrupted. "We can leave right now. Come on, Samahd. Let's be out."

Samahd thought about what Michelle said about coming in at a sensible hour.

"Can I holla at you for a minute, BJ?" Samahd pulled his ace to the side and away from the group. "I don't know about this, Cuz."

"Come on, man," BJ pleaded. "If you bail, that might fuck it up for everybody else. Just chill for a little while, then you can sneak out. Do it for the fellas."

"All right."

"Fellas!" BJ called. "Let's ride. Shameka and Rochelle, y'all can ride with us."

"I guess that leaves you and me," Abdule said to Rasheeda as he grinned. He grabbed her by the hand and led the four couples out of the party. "That's mine."

Rasheeda looked to see what car he was pointing at. Her jaw dropped when she found that it was the pearl white Porsche 911.

"Now *that's* a car," Rasheeda moaned.

"That's nothing compared to your looks, Rasheeda."

After seeing Abdule's car, the rest of the girls became curious about the cars the others drove.

"You two niggas always got to show off," Abdule laughed as he noticed where BJ and Samahd parked. The ladies missed the joke and stood looking at each other in confusion. Samahd filled them in.

"You just jealous cuz we got the best parking spots. Those belong to us."

"Y'all dudes ain't playin' no games," Shameka responded as she high-fived her girls.

"It's just a little friendly competition among friends," CT replied with a smile on his face. "Come on, Monique, let's go."

"Y'all follow me since my car's the fastest. Just make sure you keep up."

"Yeah, right," BJ laughed.

CT led Monique to his dark purple SS Chevelle, opened the door for her, then hopped in. CT took off as the rest followed close behind. He jumped on Hwy 78 and pressed the pedal to the floor. The car's take off threw them both back as the four-barrel carb opened up. The four cars raced down the highway at top speeds. CT led them to a Portuguese restaurant and pulled in. Once everyone else got there, he taunted the other three drivers because he'd arrived first.

"What happened to y'all back there?" CT taunted.

"Aww, shut up," Samahd laughed as he got out of the car. "You're the only one that knew where we were going."

"You should of figured it out," Monique

grinned as she kissed CT.

"Anyway . . . Let's go inside. Sangria on me."

While Samahd sat in the restaurant, he couldn't get Michelle off of his mind. They all sat at the table enjoying each other's conversation and company.

"I need to go to the ladies' room," Rasheeda said looking at the girls. They caught her drift and accompanied her to the bathroom. Rasheeda walked in first and pulled out a bundle. "Come on, girls. I need to get right. I'm goin' all out on these niggas."

"Let me get that," Monique said as Rasheeda pulled off a pack and a straw out of her pocket. "I only need a one on one."

"Not me," Shameka interrupted. "Gimme another bag. I'm getting ready to get right for this pretty nigga." The girls laughed.

"Girl, you silly as hell. I can't front, though. They all look good."

After they finished snorting, they cleaned up and returned to the table.

The guys sat at the table thinking about what they were going to do when CT broke the silence.

"Man," CT began, "I'm getting ready to take this broad to the Garden State Motel right quick and knock her big ass off."

"That sounds like the move," Samahd interjected. "But I can't go to the room. I have something important I have to do."

"Like what?" Abdule questioned.

"I promised Michelle I'd come home early tonight so she could cook."

"Boy, let me find out you whipped," Abdule laughed. "How in the hell can one of the richest niggas in Newark be stuck on one broad?"

"It's not like that, Big Cuz. You know my situation. I'm just trying to keep her happy. That's all."

"I can feel that, Young Blood," CT commented "What you gonna tell Shameka?"

"I'm going to tell her that I got some important business to take care of. The real question is: Who wants two bad chicks for them tonight?"

"Don't even sweat it," BJ chimed in. "I got it all under control. I'ma show these two old dudes right here how you put it down."

"Boy, you a fool," Samahd laughed as he dapped up his right-hand man. "I'm out." As Samahd got up to leave, he noticed the girls returning to the table. "Damn, I shoulda been gone. Now I gotta explain myself to this broad."

The girls floated into the room.

"Okay," Monique began. "What else do you have in store for us tonight?"

"Well," Abdule chuckled, "we thought about droppin' by the liquor store, then going to snatch up a suite. If that's okay with you."

"Damn right," Rasheeda approved.

"Then let's blow this joint." The four guys tossed money onto the table for the bill, then escorted the ladies outside.

"Hey, Shameka," Samahd broke in, "I need you to ride with BJ."

"Why? What's up?"

"Something came up and I have to go."

"That's cool with me, but you know that once we get to the room, anything goes."

"I can respect that, but dig this. That's my li'l brother. Make sure you take care of him."

"Believe me," Shameka replied with a grin on her face, "we will. He'll have plenty of things to tell you tomorrow."

"I'm sure he will." Samahd jumped in his car and rode off.

9

YOU SAID WHAT

"Donna!" Michelle called from the kitchen. "Can you come here for a minute?"

"What do you want?" Donna asked as she walked into the kitchen.

"Look in the cabinet and hand me the sugar."

"Who you cookin' all this food for?"

"None of your business, but if you must know, it's for me and Samahd."

"Why you all stuck on that boy, anyway? You know he might have had something to do with Red getting killed."

"So what if he did, Donna? Did you forget what Red did to me? On top of that, he disowned my child before he was even alive. How would you feel if that woulda happened to you?"

"Maybe you're right."

"Of course I'm right. Now where are you going tonight?"

"I was thinking about going to see Sadeek or something."

"That's cool, but make sure he keeps his business to himself. You know he sees Samahd every day."

"I can understand that, but on another note, you need to tell Samahd about you gettin' high."

"Well, on another note, I think you need

to shut the fuck up and mind your own business."

"You ain't gotta act like that wit' ya fat ass." Donna smiled at Michelle and walked out of the kitchen.

"Go to hell with your triflin' ass," Michelle hollered at her as she laughed.

Samahd pulled up to Michelle's house and parked behind her car. As he jumped out, Donna was coming out of the house.

"Hey, Samahd," Donna greeted.

"Where you goin', Li'l Miss Lady?"

"To see a friend of mine, Big Brother."

Samahd smiled at the thought of being married to Michelle one day.

"That would be nice, wouldn't it, Li'l Sis?"

"Yes, it would because then, you could start giving your little sista some money."

"Here." Samahd reached into his pocket and pulled out a wad of money. "How about we start early. Take this." He handed Donna the whole thing.

"*That's* what I'm talkin' about. Now I see why Michelle love you so much."

"I don't think she loves me for my money."

"Well, that's a damn good reason, if you ask me."

"I'll see you later, Donna. You too crazy for me." Samahd was going to knock, but the door was open. He called to Michelle as he walked into the house.

"I'm in the kitchen," she responded.

Samahd made his way into the kitchen. "There you are, pretty lady. I thought you'd be finished by now."

"I thought you'd be late, so I started late so it would be hot for you."

"You need me to help you?"

"I got it, baby. I'm almost finished. All I need to do is put the biscuits in the oven, then I can rest for about 10 or 15 minutes."

"Okay . . . I guess I'll just go in the den and watch TV."

"Make yourself comfortable. I'll bring the food in when it's ready."

The next morning Samahd woke up early, and Michelle awakened as Samahd got ready to hit the block.

"I'm sorry," he apologized and kissed Michelle on the forehead. "I didn't mean to wake you. Go back to sleep and get some rest. I got a lot of running around to do today."

"Okay, baby. Just be careful."

"I will. Go back to sleep."

Thirty minutes later, Samahd pulled on Mapes in front of Ruth's house. G Boss was sitting on the steps asleep when he got out.

"Wake yo ass up! What are you doin' sleepin' on the porch?"

"Damn," G Boss replied groggily. "I must've fell asleep waitin' on you or BJ to show up."

"Get up and go to the front of the block. Make sure everybody's ready when I come back out."

Samahd walked into the house and walked to the back room to see what had been done. Ruth got the girls to break down all 10 blocks. They were packaged in five bundled bricks. He smiled and turned to go find Ruth.

When he opened the door she was sprawled across the bed looking as ravishing as ever. Her light brown complexion gleamed from the little bit of sunshine that peeked through her window. Samahd noticed her legs were cocked open, more than likely from playing with her pussy before she fell asleep. He snuck between her legs and stuck his tongue in her sweet spot, waking her from her sleep.

"Mmmm," Ruth moaned. "You can always wake me up like that."

"I knew that would get your attention. What time did the girls finish last night?"

"They finished quick as hell. They said they had somewhere important to go."

"Damn . . . They probably wanted to go to the pool party. I didn't get a chance to see them out there. I left early. What time did they leave?"

"I don't know, Samahd. Probably around ten or eleven."

"All right then, get some sleep. I'm getting ready to hit the block to catch the early-morning rush."

Samahd went back into the room, grabbed the bricks, and walked outside to meet G Boss, who was sitting on the porch when he walked out the door. "Take these two. I'm gettin' ready to put the rest of these up. Go up to Bergen and get it jumping. Take this extra bundle for sample and let me know how they like it."

"Ok, Big Cuz. I got you. Just let me hit this first bag and I'm on my way." G Boss opened the bag and took a hit only to be blown away. "Damn, Samahd! This new shit is strong as hell. I might only need a bundle for the day and sell the rest. Shit . . . I might just make some money today."

"You a fool," Samahd laughed. "Let me

put this shit up 'for the police pull up."

"All right . . . I'm going to the front to get this off. They might try to kill me over this shit."

Samahd walked to the back to stash his bricks and came back out front. When he walked out of the alley, BJ was pulling up. He smiled because he knew he had a story to tell about the night before.

BJ hopped out of his car walking with a new stride. He was smiling as he made his way to Samahd. "You're not gonna believe what happened last night."

"Come on, man, don't start."

"Last night was the best night of my life! Ya girl, Shameka, a fool wit' hers. I put that on my 'G.' Don't get me wrong, Rochelle was an animal, but Shameka went in. She sucked any and everything you could think of. I hit them bitches until about an hour ago. Hell, I just dropped them off on my way here."

"I knew you was gonna have a story for me," Samahd laughed, playfully punching him in the stomach. "Come on. Let's go get something to eat. Lemme tell G Boss where I put them other things at before we go."

BJ and Samahd looked up the street and saw G Boss running up and down Mapes like a chicken with his head cut off.

"Yo G!" BJ called up the block.

G Boss ran top speed to BJ and Samahd.

"You look like you on a mission. Samahd must've gave you a bundle."

"I just had one bag. This shit strong as hell. I hope y'all got a bunch because I'm hustlin' all day."

"Listen," Samahd laughed, "we going to get something to eat. You want something?"

"Hell no. Just bring me back a coffee and some cigarettes from the Stop 1."

"All right. Them other thangs in the garage behind that broken brick on the left." Samahd and BJ walked off. Before long they were at their favorite spot. Abdule was sitting at his usual table in the back.

"What's going on, Abdule?" Samahd greeted as they sat down.

"I'm cool, Li'l Cuz. I'm just coming from droppin' off that broad from last night. I'm telling you, Samahd, she liked to killed me last night." BJ and Samahd laughed.

"I told you them broads got down," BJ cosigned.

"I don't wanna hear another word about them broads," Samahd replied. "On the real, Ab, you said you needed to talk to me. Let's talk."

"Samahd, I need to know if you had

anything to do with D Roc's little man getting killed. I just don't think it's a coincidence that somebody would raise their voice at you and end up dead the next day, especially when BJ was right there. D Roc been sweatin' me about it because he swears you did it."

"Between me and you, Ab . . . yeah, I did it. He broke all the rules with not a bit of respect for me. When I went to go meet with him and D Roc, he was completely outta order. D Roc had no control over him. I could tell he was going to make himself a problem. That wasn't why I did it, though. The reason I had to do it was because he put his hands on my lady."

Abdule sat in silence for a moment before he spoke. "I understand why you did what you did, but what do we do about D Roc?"

"He can never know since he couldn't control the problem in the first place."

"That makes sense. I'll just tell 'em you didn't have anything to do with it and leave it alone."

"I appreciate that. The way things are going, we don't need no hard feelings. That's bad for business."

D Roc sat on Springfield Avenue at the diner talking to Taywan.

"Look, Young Blood, I need you to step up on the lookouts and the money flow. Red was pushin' six figures through that block every week, and I need you to continue that."

"I got you, Big Dog."

"I know you got me, but I need you to understand why I'm telling you this. Red got a lot of money, but he spent it recklessly. I want you to crank it up, but I also want you to set an example for your brothers."

"I understand where you're coming from. On another note, have you found any information about who killed Red?"

D Roc stared into the distance thinking to himself, *Not only do I have a clue; I know who did it.*

"D Roc?" Taywan called, breaking his train of thought.

"Not yet but I'm on top of it. I'm just hopeful that you step it up and make a good general, Taywan. Use your head and you won't have a problem with anything else."

"I appreciate the opportunity, D Roc. I won't let you down."

"It's cool, and to show you how cool, I'm gonna start you off with a whole thang. Just bring me back 40 thousand and we straight. Do you need me to have it cut for you?"

"Nah, I got it. I'm gonna show you how I

do things on the block."

"That's what I'm talking about. Go to the car and grab one and lock the door. I'll be on the block later to check you out."

Weeks passed as Samahd flourished in the streets. He took over more and more blocks. He stood on Mapes to make sure the young ones stayed on point chasing car after car. Sadeek walked up the block toward Samahd as he stood there talking to one of his newest block runners.

"What's shakin', Samahd?" Sadeek greeted as he approached.

"Nothin' much. Just talking to one of my new go-getters. Tranel, this is my man, Sadeek."

"Nice to meet you," Tranel replied.

"Nice to meet you, too. Listen, Samahd, I need half a joint, and I was wondering what you could do for me."

"Let me ask you a question, Sadeek. Are you tryna get rich or go home early?"

"What you mean?"

"Are you tryna get rich or play with this money? Your block is next to mine, and I want to know, are you with me or against me?"

"Come on, Samahd. You know I'm with

you. I'm tryna get rich. I'd love to get fresh every day. Nigga, look at you. Between you and BJ, I don't know who da freshest."

"I can dig it," Samahd laughed. "I should have brought the proposition to you a lot sooner, and for that I apologize. Now I have something for you. You give me 17 thousand for the half, and I'm going to give you a whole one for 35 within a two-week period. The only thing I ask you is not to cut it so much, and you can keep the label. Tranel, run down to Ruth's and tell her to give you one and a half. She might not believe you, so tell her to come out and look down the street and I'll wave."

"Okay, Samahd." Tranel headed up the block.

"So, Sadeek, what's new?"

"Nothing other than coolin' with this new chick lately. Her name's Donna. She's from across town."

"Word?" Samahd smirked.

"Yes, sir, and I'm tellin' you, Cuz. She's wild."

"What do you mean she's wild?"

"Trust what I say. She suck from the rootie to the tootie."

"Get the fuck outta here. Donna snort on the low?"

"Hell, yeah! She goes crazy when she get

that blue magic in her system. How do you know her anyway, or should I say, how long have you known her?"

"I know her sister, Michelle."

"Oh, okay, I know who you're talkin' about. I met her on Lehigh and Bergen one day talkin' to their brother."

"Let me ask you a question,Sadeek. Is Michelle gettin' high, too?"

"I don't know about now, but she was back then. I just hadn't seen her in a while."

"Are you sure? The reason why I ask is because she's dear to me."

"Samahd, understand this. No one is perfect, so you can't blame her for the past."

"You may be right."

Ruth interrupted the conversation when she called Samahd's name from up the block. Samahd looked up the hill and gave her the wave of approval. She gave Tranel the bag and walked back in the house. Seconds later, Tranel made it back down the hill and gave the bag to Sadeek. "Thanks for the information."

"All right, Samahd. I'll get at you sooner than later with the funds."

"Don't worry. It's cool. Just try your best to meet the deadline."

"See you later and thanks for giving me this once-in-a-lifetime chance."

Sadeek turned down Lehigh as Samahd watched and replayed what Sadeek had told him. *How could I not know Michelle was getting high without me catching the signs?* As he stood there with a thousand thoughts racing through his head, BJ pulled up and interrupted his train of thought.

"What's up?" BJ greeted. "You all right? You look like you just seen a ghost."

"I just heard the craziest news."

"What?"

"Did you know that Donna got high?"

"Hell no! Who told you that?"

"You would not believe who's smashing her."

"Who?"

"Sadeek."

"Get the hell outta here."

"That's my word."

"Damn . . . I woulda never thought her pretty, red ass could get high."

"Yeah, I know. He said that Michelle been gettin' high, too."

"Wow," BJ expressed with surprise. "Now I know what you're thinking and don't start."

"That's the same thing Sadeek said."

"What are you gonna do?"

"First, we got this meeting tonight. As far

as Michelle is concerned, I'm just gonna keep my eye on her for a couple of days."

"Besides the meeting, what else is in the mix for tonight?"

"I don't know. I heard there's a party out in Elizabeth that's supposed to be jumpin'."

"Sounds like a plan to me. Let's get to this meeting."

Michelle and Donna stood outside of the mall getting ready to go in to shop for baby clothes for her soon-to-be baby boy.

"Come on, Donna," Michelle demanded. "Stop putting that shit in your nose."

"Don't act funny, bitch. You still get down, too."

"Just come on and stop running your big-ass mouth."

"Stop being bossy, fat girl," Donna joked. "And you better be buying me something with all that money."

"I might if you help me pick out something for my son to wear home from the hospital."

"I got so excited when the doctor said you were having a boy. I almost cried."

"Did you even notice my reaction when she said that?"

"Notice it? I had to calm your stankin' ass down."

Samahd and BJ walked into the Robert Treat Motel to catch the meeting. Samahd was the first to walk through the conference-room door.

"What's shakin', fellas?" Samahd greeted. "I hope I haven't missed anything or ruffled any feathers for being late."

D Roc looked up and despised Samahd for his arrogance.

"No, Samahd," Abdule began. "You haven't missed anything. As a matter of fact, we were just starting, and you're the main subject for tonight." They all knew that the consequence for being late to a meeting. It would cost $10,000 and last pick of the batch. Yet, Abdule looked over this for Samahd.

"Our shipment has picked up significantly, thanks to Samahd and the blocks he runs. His branch has moved from 20 to 40 keys every two weeks. He has set a new standard for us all, and we should be grateful for his contributions, as well as, his loyalty to us all. I'm not asking everyone to do this because that would be asking too much from some of us. I'm just bringing this to everyone's attention because anyone that pushes himself will be taken care of. I just want to say that I'm thankful for having Samahd and BJ, so we're going to celebrate my decision of making Samahd my right-hand man. Are there any objections about my decision?"

D Roc sat there trying his best not to object. He knew everyone would know that he felt hatred for Samahd if he said anything. He stood by, heated at the entire situation at hand.

"Now that that's outta the way, does anyone have any idea where we can go to party?"

"I do," BJ interjected. "Let's go to Elizabeth."

"Sounds good to me," approved CT. "Let's go shut it down."

"Then it is agreed. Elizabeth it is. Meeting adjourned."

Later on that night, they all made it to the club in Elizabeth around 12:30. D Roc decided to bring Taywan with him. The party was so packed that no one else could get in. Abdule walked up to the bouncer and handed him $5,000 and instructed him to let him and his boys in. Without hesitation, the bouncer cleared the way. Before they all made it in, someone called Ab's name. It was Rasheeda from the pool party.

"What's up, baby girl?"

"I'm cool, Big Daddy, but I'm with all my girls, and they won't let us in."

"How many you got?"

"It's about 11 of us. Look over there."

Abdule looked in the direction Rasheeda was pointing and lost his mind looking at the herd of stallions. He turned back to the bouncer and gave him another $2,000 for the girls. The bouncer shrugged his shoulders and let the ladies in. Once inside the club, Abdule caught up with Samahd and the rest of the fellas.

Rasheeda walked up behind BJ and whispered in his ear. "I have a surprise for you and the rest of the fellas."

BJ turned around and saw all the women, including the girls from the pool party.

"You had this shit planned the whole time," BJ said to Abdule.

"Nah, but you know we gettin' ready to get it in now."

"Who are all these bad broads?" D Roc asked Abdule.

"That's right . . . I forgot you weren't at the pool party. You'll get to know them soon enough."

"I'd rather sooner than later," D Roc laughed as they walked to the bar in the VIP section. D Roc handed the bartender $10,000 and informed him that there was no limit.

Samahd and one of the other Kings, Rashon, also known as Ra, walked through the club to check out the scene. The club was packed so tight they could hardly move. Ra was trying to get around someone, but he wouldn't move.

"Excuse me, Fam." Samahd was standing right behind him. "I said, excuse me, Fam. I'm tryna get through." He still didn't move so Ra pushed past him.

"Yo!" the dude barked. "Watch where the fuck you goin', Nigga."

"Who the fuck you talkin' to?" Ra fired back.

"I'm talkin' to you, Motherfucka. You the only one bumpin' into me."

Ra turned to walk away and spun back around with a strong right-left combo to the stomach and face. As Ra and the dude squared off, Samahd caught him from behind knocking him to the floor. His homeboy came from behind Samahd and kicked him in the stomach, knocking the wind out of him.

"This bitch kicked me!"

Before Samahd could gather his senses, BJ came through and dropped the dude that kicked Samahd, then caught the other dude with an uppercut, sending them both to the floor.

"What the fuck y'all fight for and we got all these broads ready to get it in?" BJ yelled over the music.

"Nigga tried to play me and Samahd so we had to go to work."

"I can see that—" Before BJ could finish his sentence one of the dudes popped off the floor with a knife, hitting BJ in the torso.

"That's it!" Samahd yelled. "Party's over!" He pulled out his .38 snub and squeezed one right in the face of the guy that stabbed BJ. "Come on, BJ. We gotta go!"

They made their way through the crowd to the VIP. Ra made it back first.

"Shit just got real. We gotta go. Me and Samahd got into it with some niggas, BJ got stabbed, and Samahd popped somebody."

"Let's go!" Abdule commanded. "Grab BJ."

Taywan took BJ from Samahd as they all headed to the front door. D Roc and Samahd were the only two holding heat, so they took front line as Ra cleared the way. Shots fired out from all directions. They fired back into the crowd.

"I *love* this shit!" D Roc shouted as he fired shots. "Y'all got the whole Elizabeth shootin' at us."

Abdule told Rochelle to get into the car with BJ so she could drive. Everybody else jumped in a car with somebody. Samahd and D Roc were the last two that made it to their cars. The last two girls jumped in with them as the police came flying onto the scene. The police cars got caught directly in the fire coming from the Elizabeth boys while the Kings of Newark sped off safely out of harm's way.

When they were far enough away, they pulled into White Castle on Elizabeth Avenue in Newark. Samahd pulled over next to BJ's car and got out.

"You all right?"

"Hell, no! I done messed up my damn linen shirt." They laughed.

"You crazy as hell," Ra joked. "First, I see you knock a nigga out, then you get stabbed and curse a nigga out. You a wild dude."

"You tryna go to the hospital?" Samahd asked.

"Nope. I'm tryna wrap this shit up to stop the bleeding, then get me some pussy."

"Boy, you retarded," Rochelle smirked.

"What now?" Monique asked Abdule.

"We still got the motel for tonight. We can take the party over there."

"Then let's go," Shameka approved as she latched onto Samahd's arm. "I'm finally with my baby. This time. I'm not letting him get away."

* * *

Donna and Sadeek walked out of the movie theater in North Newark.

"How was the movie?" Sadeek asked as he draped his arm around her.

"It was real nice." Donna paused for a moment. "Why are you being so nice to me all of a sudden?"

"No reason. I'm just doing a little better these days."

"And how are you doing that?"

"I got down with my man, Samahd."

"You work for Samahd now?"

"What's wrong with that?"

"Nothing . . . it's just that he's my sister's man."

"Word? I did not know that. I just told him about you and Michelle's li'l secret."

"What the fuck do you mean?"

"I just told him that you and Michelle get high. I didn't know they were that close."

"Well, you shoulda thought about that before you ran your big-ass mouth about me and my sister's business. Now I have to tell Michelle that Samahd knows she gets high. How could you do something like this?"

"I'm sorry, Donna. That was my bad. I

just hope that this won't hinder our friendship."

"I don't know, Sadeek. Just take me home. Right now!"

"Are you sure you're not mad at me?"

"Of course, I'm mad at you! You just told my sister's baby's father that she gets high."

"What did you say?"

"Michelle is pregnant by Samahd."

"I think I fucked up."

"You think?"

10

2 WEEKS LATER

Two weeks had passed since the shootout in Elizabeth. Things were rolling smooth for Samahd and his growing empire. A warm Thursday afternoon found Samahd and Ra pulling into a Pontiac dealership. It was around 2:30. They walked through the front door with Samahd in the front.

"Good day, gentlemen," a salesman greeted. "May I help you with something?"

"I'm looking at this GTO right here."

"That is a fine piece of machinery."

"I see that, but I have a question. Can you have your personnel take the governor off so it would hold back?"

"Of course, I can, if you're willing to pay the price."

"Pay the price?" Samahd laughed as he elbowed Ra. "Take this." Samahd threw the salesman two stacks of money. "That's $50,000. That should be enough and take those alloys off and find me some chrome."

"Yes, sir. Right away. When would you like for us to have it ready for you."

"By the end of the day. Will that be a problem?"

"Not at all, sir. Thank you for the generous tip."

"You're welcome. Remember my face because I'll be back." Samahd and Ra turned to walk out.

D Roc cruised onto Prince Street to check out how Taywan was doing. He pulled over when he saw him standing in front of a store.

"Taywan!" D Roc called as he rolled down the window. "How's everything?" They exchanged greetings as D Roc got out of the car.

"Take a look around for yourself, Big Dog."

D Roc looked around to observe what was going on around the Prince Street Projects. Cars moved back and forth with soldiers running up and down the street, in and out of buildings, moving brick after brick.

"Now that you've said something, Taywan, things are looking great."

"Thanks, D. I'm working hard to get things right."

"I can dig that. You're definitely doing your thing. How's it going over in New Community?"

"It's even better over there because it's already very established. We don't have anything to worry about. Everything is moving along as planned."

BJ and Tranel sat on Mapes while they watched young homies move up and down Bergen catching fiend after fiend. Ra pulled up on Mapes behind BJ's car and let Samahd out. BJ got out and walked around to the driver's side to greet Ra.

"What's good with you?" BJ greeted as he gave Ra a pound.

"Nah, what's good with yo' crazy ass?"

"I'm just chillin'."

"Did you ever go get that stab wound looked at?"

"Hell, no! You know Beth Israel is the cause of 80 percent of the deaths in Newark." The two laughed. "But on the real, I didn't need it. I feel like Rochelle healed me after I tore that pussy up about three times."

Sadeek walked up the block on Lehigh and saw John talking on the corner. As he looked closer, he noticed that John looked mad. He knew John was Michelle and Donna's only brother. *This nigga better have my money*, he thought to himself as he continued to walk toward John. When he got there, Sadeek jumped right in the middle of the conversation.

"What's up, Li'l Cuz? How you?"

"Nigga, I'm good, but what the fuck's up

with you is the question."

"What do you mean what's up with me? You and my money is all I care about."

"Fuck you and your money! What the hell are you doing tellin' my sisters' business?"

"That business ain't got shit to do with this business."

"First of all, anything that has to do with my family is my business. Second of all—" John didn't finish his sentence before he hit Sadeek with a quick uppercut-left hook combo knocking him to the pavement. "Now mind your own business, Nigga!" G Boss saw the whole thing happen and ran to get Samahd.

He saw Samahd, Tranel, and BJ standing on the Backstreet. "Samahd!" he called. "I need you right quick."

"What's wrong, G Boss?"

"John just knocked Sadeek out."

"Come on, BJ. Let's go get this dude before he makes us look bad."

"It's a little late for that," G Boss laughed.

When they got there, Sadeek was getting up off of the ground.

"You all right?" Samahd grinned.

"I'm good. Li'l Cuz over there snuck me while I wasn't paying attention."

John heard what Sadeek said and got mad

all over again.

"It didn't ever go down like that," John snarled. "This motherfucka need to mind his own business. He's all in my family shit cuz he fucked Donna!"

"Hold up," Samahd calmed him down. "Slow down for a minute. Now *you're* telling the family business. What's the meaning of you putting your hands on him?"

"He's the one that told you about Michelle and now she's at Mom's all upset."

"I feel where you're coming from. Just calm down. Take a ride with me. I need to go pick up my car." Turning to BJ, he said, "Get this shit under control while I'm gone. Sadeek . . . tighten up and get some order around here."

Samahd and John walked around the corner, jumped in Samahd's Cadillac, and headed back to the Pontiac dealership. As they rode, the thought of John becoming a brother to him crossed his mind. He knew he had to do something to gain his trust and confidence. When they got to the dealership, Samahd decided to let John be the first one to drive his new car. He gave him the keys and told him to follow him to his mother's house.

Michelle sat on the front porch with

Donna enjoying the last of the summer breeze.

"Girl," Donna began, "you're getting big as hell."

"You're getting big and you ain't even pregnant."

"Don't hate me because I'm beautiful."

"Yeah, right," Michelle laughed. "If you're beautiful, then I'm a goddess." The two sisters laughed as Michelle noticed a car speeding up the block. "Who's that?"

"I don't know, but he's pulling up right here."

John pulled up in front of his mother's house; Samahd came gliding up the street and pulled up behind him. Samahd jumped out as smooth as a baby's bottom and slid to the porch like a pimp.

"Hey, baby," Samahd greeted as he kissed Michelle and sat down beside her. "What's up, Donna? You okay, baby? You look upset."

"I'm all right."

"You will not believe what your brother did on the block today."

"What did you do, John?" Michelle asked.

"What?" John smirked. "It wasn't my fault."

"This nigga put them thangs on Sadeek."

"You pulled a gun out on Sadeek?"
Donna asked.

"They might as well been guns the way
they laid him out."

"Why would you do that, John?"
Michelle scolded. "As much as Sadeek has
looked out for you."

"Because he ran his mouth and told
Samahd about you gettin' high. That wasn't for
him to tell. That was between you and
Samahd." Michelle put her head down.

"It's okay, baby," Samahd consoled her.
"You just should've told me before I had to
hear it from somebody else. We can get past
this."

"I just felt like you woulda been
disgusted with me had I told you."

"You mean the world to me, Michelle.
I'm serious. You're not some random chick out
here in these streets. You're my lady. The same
lady that I wanna give my last name to one
day."

"Yeah, right," Michelle laughed. "Don't
be tryna gas my head up like I'm one of your
groupies you got runnin around Newark. By the
way, whose car is that?"

"That's just something I picked up."

11

JOHN'S TURN

Samahd and John sat in the kitchen eating breakfast.

"Listen, John," Samahd began as he paused from his breakfast, "I want you to move over to Mapes where it's a lot busier. The only thing is that it takes more responsibility."

"What do you mean?"

"You have to be on top of your game at all times, and you need more protection."

"So what you sayin'?"

"I keep my pistol on me at all times."

"Okay, I got you."

"I'm going to stay wit' Michelle for a while. If you need to get back, take the Caddy."

"*That's* what's up." John finished eating and left the house to run some errands for his mother.

Later on that day, John hit the block. When he pulled onto Mapes, BJ noticed he was driving Samahd's car.

"What up, Cuz?" BJ greeted. "Where's Samahd?"

"He's at the crib chillin' wit' Michelle."

"Michelle bringin' him back?"

".Nah . . . he just picked up a GTO."

"That nigga think he slick," BJ laughed. "He gon' make me step my game up."

"True, indeed. Oh yeah, Samahd wants

me to move over here, so I guess I'm under you."

"That's what's up. Check this out. More than likely it's gon' be me, you, Tranel, and G Boss. That don't include the young runners. We the strongest team in Newark because we all work together. We work hard and play hard, you feel me?"

"I can work that." As the conversation came to a close, Abdule slid up on a motorcycle.

"What's good, BJ?" Abdule greeted. "What's the deal for the day?"

"I can't call it. What's up with you?"

"Just playin' the city right now."

"I see. I like that Harley right there."

"Where ya boy at?"

"He chillin' with his girl. He should be out later on."

"Dig that. Tell 'em I rolled through."

"Will do. We'll probably get into somethin' tonight."

"Just holla at me. You know where I'm at." Abdule revved the engine and pulled off.

Turning back to John, BJ said, "Let's walk up the block so I can give you something and fill you in on what's what." The two headed up Mapes to Ruth's house.

D Roc and Taywan sat on Prince Street talking about what's been going on in the hood.

"What's been going on?" Taywan asked D Roc.

"Listen here, man. I feel kinda funny about that nigga, Samahd."

"Why you say that?"

"I can almost swear that he had something to do with Red's murder."

"Get the fuck outta here."

"I'm serious. He's the only one that coulda pulled something off like that so smoothly. You already know him and Red got into it right before he got killed."

"I didn't know that."

"At first I had to let it pass because of Red's violation."

"What violation?"

"Samahd brought the situation to the Four Kings earlier about his girl. Abdule made it so that I could get them together to talk things out for the better of business. The next day, they got into an argument over Samahd's girl. Now this nigga running around gettin' rich while my man is in the dirt."

"That's some bullshit. What you wanna do? That's my word, Roc. I will touch this nigga."

"I know, but listen. There's no way I can be involved in this because of the Kings. I would be in direct violation, punishable by death on sight. I need you to understand how complicated this is."

"I can make sure that you have nothing to do with it."

"In that case, get it done."

"How do you think I can catch him?"

"The first thing you need to do is send him a message. Samahd's a smart nigga. He will beef up the protection on his blocks. The only way you can really catch him is in his car."

"I'll get it rolling tonight."

"That's cool. Just make sure you send the right message because it could very well cost you your life."

Samahd blazed through Elizabeth Avenue in the silver bullet on his way to Mapes when he noticed Abdule on the corner of Meeker and Elizabeth. He pulled over to where he was. Abdule could do nothing but shake his head.

"Why you always gotta show your ass?" Abdule laughed.

"Just a little something I picked up."

"She clean as hell. So what's the plan for tonight?"

"Me and the homies might step out for a couple of drinks or something."

"Sounds like a plan. Just holla at me so I can slide through."

"That's a dolla bet."

BJ and John walked out of Ruth's house as BJ explained some things to him. "All you got to do with the 20 bricks I gave you is pass them out to some of the li'l homies. Charge them no more than 350 because they all know what we charge. I usually charge 'em 300. Tranel pays 250, which is half and half. The 20 I gave you are yours to keep. You don't owe me nothing on them. Samahd already called Ruth and let her know what the deal is. When you finish those, it's 200 to re-up."

"Damn, Cuz. I really appreciate this. You got my loyalty and my all. That's my word."

As John and BJ were finishing business, Samahd rolled up in the GTO and hopped out fresh to death.

"What's it looking like, BJ?"

"Everything good in the hood. We just gettin' ready to go celebrate John's coming over to the main blocks."

"What you got in mind?"

"Nothing special. We can go to Roland's and chop it up."

The three sat outside watching the block move until night fell. John put his block skills to work early by finding two fast runners. Samahd overheard him telling them that they owed him 300, but if they finished the same day, they only owed him 280. Samahd chuckled to himself because John reminded him of himself.

"Hey, Samahd," John called. "I appreciate them 20. If I get rid of all of them today or tomorrow, I'll be ready to re-up. Some I'm gonna sell myself and try to make 500 while I'm on my heavy grind. To make a long story short, I should have at least $6,000 for you tomorrow."

"If that's the case," BJ began, "you give the six and I'll throw you 20 more on top of the 20 you get. All you gotta do is pay the rest of your bill, which will be $2,000 more than what you should have. I already know your profit margin, so you should have $10,000 by the end of the week. I hope you can do it because the only person I've ever seen do that is Samahd, but he didn't have no help." Samahd turned to BJ and smiled because he was thinking the same thing.

"All right, fellas," Samahd chuckled. "That's enough for today. Let's go down to Roland's and get some drinks on me."

"Shit, if you payin', I'm drinkin' the whole bar," BJ laughed.

"Hold up before you leave," John interjected. "Let me go get my pistol."

12

THE GET BACK

Taywan had gathered a crew of skilled killers to get at Samahd. "Listen up," he began, "I got an extra $50,000 for the man that actually kills Samahd. This is a picture of him so you'll know your main target." Taywan passed the picture around. "I want you all to understand this. No one is to know who's behind this. If you get caught, your fate is death. Understand?"

"Yeah," they replied in unison.

"Good. Let's get rid of some old, dirty laundry."

They all left and jumped in their cars ready to carry out their orders and cash in on a bonus, if possible.

Samahd, BJ, John, and Tranel walked down Bergen Street laughing about the events that happened through the day. Tranel stopped on Shepherd Avenue to get some weed from Smiley. Smiley was young, but he was a basketball star. He was already 6'2" in his sophomore year in high school.

"What's up, Tranel?" Smiley greeted as he stood dribbling a basketball. "What it look like?"

"I'm good. Let me get 10 nicks of that Golden Crush."

"Bet. What y'all gettin' into tonight?"

"Nothin' much. Me, Samahd, and BJ gettin' it in."

"Let's go then. I got 3 bags on the cypha."

"Let's roll then."

Samahd, BJ, and John walked into Roland's to find a party that was already jumping. Samahd sent BJ to the bar to get the shots ready while he and John walked back outside to wait on Tranel. When they got outside, John saw Tranel and Smiley walking into the Chinese store across the street.

"I'm going across the street to get Tranel," John informed Samahd.

"All right . . . I'll be right here."

As John walked across the street, Samahd noticed an unfamiliar red Cutlass riding slow down Bergen. John noticed the same car as he was walking. He drew his gun as soon as he got across the street. Before he could draw, they found their primary target. Samahd's last sight was a man in a red do-rag brandishing his weapon. Sparks flew everywhere as Samahd tried to make his move, but it was too late. John saw the whole situation unfold and was able to run up on the car as they steadily moved up Bergen. He released shots, disabling the driver.

BJ heard the shots from outside and ran

to the door. Tranel came out of the store releasing his tre pound. The car took so many shots it was full of holes. As BJ came out the door to join his two soldiers, two men managed to jump from the moving vehicle. They closed in on the two as they backed down. John moved around the car and rose from the rear of the two men, hitting one in the leg. Tranel came from behind another car after reloading and saw the man cringing in pain. He had the jump on him. He fired and caught him in the shoulder, knocking him back. Out of nowhere, a brown Caprice came from around the corner and stopped, yelling for the two men to jump in. They both turned to make a break for it. John was so close to the car that the driver didn't see him. After reloading his last clip, he tried to release every shot.

"Catch him!" BJ yelled as he ran up on the car.

The wounded man fell as the other two made it to the car and sped off. BJ was furious. He walked over to the wounded soldier and put two more shots in his head. He turned and asked of Samahd's whereabouts. Tranel immediately thought of where Samahd was standing and ran to the side of the bar entrance. As he made it, he saw Samahd laid out with his foot kicking.

"Oh shit!" Tranel cried. "BJ, get over here now!"

"Fuck!" BJ shouted when he got to where his ace was lying. "John, go get the car!" John took off to get the car as BJ knelt down holding on to Samahd for dear life. In a matter of minutes, John returned. They argued about whether to move Samahd or not, then put him in the car and blazed off.

Michelle was at home talking to Donna about the week's events.

"Can you believe what John did to Sadeek?" Donna expressed.

"Girl, who you tellin'?" Michelle laughed.

"I can't believe him. He probably done messed up my damn suga daddy." As the two sisters laughed, the phone rang.

"Grab that, Donna. I gotta go to the bathroom."

"Hello?" she answered.

"Donna, it's John. Where's Michelle?"

"She's in the bathroom. What's wrong?"

"Tell her Samahd just got shot, and she needs to hurry down to Beth Israel. He only wants to see her."

"Oh my God!" Donna screamed as she

dropped the phone. "Michelle!"

"What? What's wrong?"

"Samahd's been shot. We gotta go!"

"Where is he?"

"Beth Israel."

Donna and Michelle frantically gathered their things and rushed out of the house.

"Who was responsible for watching out for Samahd?" BJ asked as he sat in the middle of the circle in the family waiting room.

"I was," John replied. "I let him know I was goin' across the street to tell Tranel we were already inside. He told me to go ahead and he was going to stand there and wait. I knew something wasn't right when I saw the car creepin' down the street."

"So what did you do?"

"I opened up, but I guess Samahd noticed it too late. I didn't even know he got hit. I tried my best to take care of the car."

"All right, then . . . I can understand that. You did good. I'll vouch for that." As BJ was talking, a nurse walked into the room.

"Samahd is doing fine. We just moved him upstairs to ICU. His mother is up there now. He asked for Michelle to come up as soon as she gets here."

"Yes, ma'am."

When the nurse walked out of the waiting room, he turned back to his men. "It's time to hit the fucking streets and get some answers before Samahd gets up and going. I at least wanna have a name for him when he gets out." As BJ instructed his men, Michelle came running through the entrance.

"Excuse me," she said frantically. "Can you please tell me where Samahd Lewis is at?"

"Yes . . . give me one moment to look it up."

As Michelle impatiently waited for the nurse to look up the information, BJ approached her from behind.

"Come on, Michelle. Let me tell you what's going on."

"Oh my God, BJ! Where's Samahd?"

"Calm down. He's up on the 3rd floor. His moms is in there with him right now. He's not in ICU no more so he should be okay. He's in Room 327."

"Thank you, BJ."

Michelle walked up to the door of Samahd's room and knocked lightly.

"Who is it?" asked Mrs. Lewis.

"It's Michelle. May I come in?"

"Yes."

Michelle poked her head in the room, and then walked in.

"I'm so glad you're here. Samahd has been asking for you all night."

"Is he okay?"

"He'll be fine. He's actually blessed. Two inches higher and the bullet would have struck his heart. He must really love you the way he's been worried about you."

"I hope so because I love him."

"Well, I'm glad to finally meet you. I'm so happy to know that my son finally has a woman in his life that cares for him."

Taywan sat in Prince Street Projects pissed at how his soldiers had failed. Only one remained alive.

"What the hell happened out there?"

"We saw Samahd standing on the block by himself as soon as we got in the area. That's when we opened up on him."

"Then what happened?"

"We didn't notice the dudes across the street. As soon as we opened up on Samahd, they opened up on us. You can see by our failure that we underestimated Samahd's loyal men."

"Never mind that. Did Samahd get shot?"

"I believe he was."

"What the fuck you mean you *believe*? Was he or was he not?"

"I saw him fall to the ground, so I know he was at least hit."

"Let's start letting our people know what's up. I'll see you later. I have a few things to take care of. Here's an extra ten grand for at least touching the target."

13
Rehab

Michelle sat in the hospital room waiting for Samahd to awake. She thought about all the good times they had together as she stood over him. Samahd opened his eyes to see her standing over him in a daze.

"Hey, baby," Samahd spoke groggily.

"Don't you ever scare me like that again. You hear me?"

"I can dig it. Shit, for that much, I hope I don't scare myself like that. Where's my mom at?"

"She went home to get some rest. I told her I'd stay here 'til you woke up. I didn't realize it was daytime. The nurse just came in and gave you some more morphine."

"Good because my stomach is killing me."

"The doctor said the bullet went straight through, so I guess that's a good thing."

"It is. That means they didn't have to go diggin' around in my body."

"You so silly."

"You gotta be silly in a situation like this."

"So what happened?"

"I really don't know. Just that someone tried to kill me."

"Are you going to be okay, because I need you here for me and our baby. When do you think enough is enough?"

"I don't know, Michelle. Just let me get everything in order."

"Well, you need to tighten up."

"You're right. Where are my clothes?"

"They threw them away because of all the blood. Your belongings are over there."

"All right then. Help me up so I can get the fuck outta here."

Michelle helped Samahd up as they got ready to leave the hospital.

BJ, John, and Tranel sat at Ruth's house trying to put and two and two together.

"Does anybody have any idea of the men that made the attempt on Samahd last night?" BJ asked.

"I don't know," John replied. "Word on the street is that one of the bodies that were found lived on Prince Street."

"Do we have anybody on Prince?" Tranel asked.

"Yes, we do, and that's what I don't understand."

"What don't you understand?"

"Taywan runs that whole strip, and he hasn't tried to contact us yet. As a matter of fact, let's go."

"Go where?"

"Over to Prince to see if we can catch Taywan."

"What if we don't see him outside?"

"What do you think?"

"I don't know."

"Then somethin' ain't right."

Michelle helped Samahd walk out of the hospital in just his gown.

"Come on, baby. I got you."

"Where the hell did you park? North Newark?"

"No, silly. I parked right on Maple."

"I feel like we been walking forever."

"There's the car right there." Michelle helped Samahd get into the car. "Where do you want to go?"

"I don't know. That's what I'm thinking about right now. It really depends on who's trying to kill me. Come to think of it, nobody knows where you live so I think that's where I'm going to stay until I heal up."

"That's cool because the doctor said you should be up and running in a few days."

"I don't think they know me too well. I'll be up and running by tomorrow. On your way to the house I need you to stop by Rite Aid and get this prescription filled."

"Let me get you to the house, and then

I'll go back out."

BJ pulled up on Prince Street to a crowd of people running back and forth.

"You see all these people out here, John? It looks like somebody from every apartment out here."

"They probably all get high."

"Come on. Let's go see if we can catch Taywan."

Taywan figured that some of Samahd's soldiers would be coming by so he made sure he was outside early.

"Make sure you finish those last two bricks before you go to school."

"I got you, Tay. Don't even worry about it."

"As a matter of fact, go get that little crowd right there coming up." Taywan took a closer look. "Them ain't no junkies. Who is it?"

"I don't know, but I'll go find out." The young blood walked toward the crowd. "Can I help you fellas?"

"I'm lookin' for Taywan," BJ answered.

"Oh yeah? And who should you be?"

"Just know that they call me BJ. Ya dig?"

"I can dig that. Give me a second and

wait right here."

"Don't take all fuckin' day."

The youngin' brushed off BJ's last comment and walked back in the hallway to Taywan.

"It's a nigga named BJ outside lookin' for you. He talkin' mad shit, too."

"Word? Don't sweat it. I'll go outside and check this nigga."

Taywan walked outside toward the men. "What's good, BJ?"

"Have you seen the news this morning?"

"Nah . . . What's up with the news?"

"They say some people from over here got killed last night."

"I ain't heard shit about it."

"You mean to tell me this whole strip is yours and nobody told you a couple of people from this project was shot last night?"

"First of all, BJ, it's 7:48 in the morning. Second of all, no one has told me anything."

"Then let me be the first to tell you that some of your soldiers died last night."

"Hold up, Blood! None of my soldiers are dead, but thank you for telling me that someone died from Prince Street."

"Look, Cuz. I didn't come down here to tongue wrestle with you. I just heard about the murders and came to pay my respects."

"Thank you for your kindness. Did they say where they got shot?"

"On Bergen."

"So you telling me your soldiers killed them."

"For some reason they opened up on us last night."

"I apologize for what happened last night, but I assure you it was none of my men. I'll get to the bottom of this."

"You do that and make sure you get back wit' me ASAP."

"I should know something no later than tomorrow night."

"Then it's settled. Get at me." BJ turned to walk away.

"Hold up, BJ. Did you lose any men?"

"Hell, no. You already know how we get down."

"Glad to hear that. I'll get at you later."

Samahd sat in the house with Michelle watching TV. "Can you make me something to eat?" he asked.

"My mother just started cooking about 15 minutes ago. I'll go see what she's cooking before the movie starts."

"I'll be right here."

"Wow, Samahd. how long is this nice person going to last?"

"As long as you would like it to."

"You are so full of it."

"I'm actually feeling a lot better. I can move on my own."

"Well, don't move too much right now."

"Okay, but tomorrow, I have to go outside and check on some things."

"That's fine. Just get some rest right now."

"Look who's talking. Your stomach look like you're about to explode."

"Who you telling? I was due *three days* ago."

"Maybe you'll have it sometime this week."

"That would be so nice. Then I can get rid of these big-ass breasts."

"Hold up, young lady. Maybe I like those big-ass breasts."

"Don't worry. You'll still love me when they're gone, along with the new addition to our little family."

"You got a point. Come gimme a kiss."

"I love you so much, Samahd."

"Michelle and Samahd," Michelle's mother called from the kitchen. "Come eat. Tell your sister to get off the phone and come in here too."

"Yes, ma'am."

14
TIME TO STRATEGIZE

John sat on Mapes the next morning making sure his new runners moved with stride.

"Yo, Tim!" John called. "Come here for a minute."

"What's up, John?"

"I've been watching you move these past couple of days, and you been bringin' in a lot of money."

"Thanks, Fam. I'm tryna get me a new G ride."

"I can dig that. I'll make you a deal. All you have to do is stay loyal to our crew and this block. Keep pumping hard and I'll buy you that car outta my own money."

"For real?"

"That's my word."

Tranel and G Boss were at Ruth's talking.

"Look, man," Tranel began, "we need to keep things in order until Samahd gets up and running again."

"I know. BJ told me the same thing earlier today. If it makes you feel any better, I only got like two bricks left of the five you gave me this morning."

"That's good because those were the last

five I had left."

"In that case, take this money right here and as soon as I finish these last two, I got you."

John walked up on the conversation.

"What's good, fellas?"

"Coolin' right now, Fam. Getting ready to smoke this blunt. How you been these past couple days?"

"Minus the bullshit, I'm good."

"I heard you put in work last night," G Boss smiled.

"Anything for the team. I woulda done the same thing for you."

Early the next morning, Samahd woke up reenergized. "Damn," Samahd said as he stretched. "My body feels so much better than it did yesterday. Hey, baby . . . did you hear me?"

"I heard you, but I'm not feeling you."

"That's fine, because it would be a surprise if you were."

"Shut up and sit your ass down somewhere."

"Can't do it. I got some running around to do before I become too weak to do it."

"Where are you going, Samahd?"

"Just to the block and a few more spots. I'll call you later and let you know I'm all right."

"Just be careful."

Samahd felt good to be behind the wheel of his own car. Driving faster and faster he maneuvered his way to Bergen. He turned on Mapes and pulled into a parking spot. As he revved his motor, he noticed Tranel, John, and G Boss sitting on the porch. He climbed out of the car with a slow stride. Tranel couldn't believe Samahd was out of recovery so fast.

"What's up, Big Cuz?" Tranel greeted. "How you living?"

"Better than ever. Better than ever."

"I can dig that."

"What's up, John? You act like you happy to see me or something." Samahd knew that John was the one that truly saved him. He walked over and gave John a hug and whispered in his ear, "I appreciate what you did for me, and I'll show you my gratitude throughout my life."

"Thanks, but it's not that serious."

"It is to me."

BJ heard all the noise outside and wondered what the commotion was. He slung the front door open in a rage. "Why the fuck does it sound like y'all havin' a party out here?" As BJ finished his sentence, he noticed Samahd sitting on the porch smiling at his general in charge.

"You make a great leader in my absence, but you need to calm it down a little bit," Samahd laughed.

"Oh shit!" BJ ran over and embraced his leader. "What's up?"

"You know me, man."

"As long as you're hurt, we're hurt."

"I know, but I'm here now so fill me in on the news and the leads you got on who tried to end my career at an early age."

Abdule sat on Elizabeth Avenue talking to one of his young soldiers.

"What's up, Young Blood? How you?"

"I'm good, Ab. What you do last night?"

"You know me. I was laid up wit' this li'l broad last night. What's been going on in the hood?"

"You know Samahd got shot a couple days ago."

"What! Who the fuck shot Samahd?"

"No one knows."

"You mean to tell me that nobody in Newark knows who shot my head nigga in charge. Get the word out now. I want a meeting with the Kings tonight. Whoever doesn't come is a suspect, so make sure you find all four."

"I'm on it right now."

Samahd and BJ put everyone to work while they sat inside of Ruth's house to talk.

"I know you have a clue of who shot me."

"I don't know how you're gonna take this, but I think D Roc and Taywan had something to do with it. One of the niggas we shot was from Prince Street. You know Taywan doesn't make a move unless D Roc says so."

"You sound more and more like me every day."

"I learned from the best."

"Sounds like you on the right track. The thing that bothers me is why did he wait for so long when he's always had a clue."

"That's a good question."

"It'll all come together soon."

BJ and Samahd got up and walked outside. As soon as they stepped on the porch, Abdul pulled up and told them that Abdule called a meeting of the Kings.

D Roc sat in the diner on Springfield Avenue as Taywan's Impala pulled up. Taywan walked in furious.

"Fuck, man!" Taywan expressed as he sat down. "I don't understand how those damn flunkies missed."

"Please, Tay, calm down. I should be the one yelling right now. First off, you missed. I told you to be precise about the situation. The first thing that came outta my mouth was that Samahd and his team were no slouches. The second thing I should be mad about is the fact that you made me hot. I done already heard that BJ came through your hood because one of the men on the news was from your block."

"I apologize for the mess I caused, but I got your back no matter what."

"I can dig that but you must understand I have to play my cards right."

"Just let me know what you need me to do."

"Right now I need you back on the block while I think. The word is already out that the Kings have a meeting tonight. I'll pick you up and we'll go from there."

15
MAJOR MEETING

Abdule sat in the Robert Treat Hotel waiting for the meeting to start.

"Come here, young blood."

"What's up, Ab?"

"Do you have any clue of what's going on around this motherfucka?"

"I mean . . . you know I hear shit. Then, of course, I think of shit myself."

"Man, stop with all that philosophy shit and let me know what's going on."

"Well, first of all, who would be strong enough to go against Samahd?"

"Most likely one of the Kings, but that doesn't tell me which King. Hold on . . ."

"I know, Ab. Let me finish. Think of the Kings. Samahd is close to Rashon and CT, so we can mark them out. Samahd and D Roc have never really liked each other. Now you tell me."

"I never really thought about it like that, but they have had a few problems, now that you mention it." As Abdule and young blood continued to talk, the rest of the Kings walked in one after the other.

"Now that everybody's here, let's get this meeting started. Today, we're here to talk about the attempt that has been brought to Samahd. Out of all four of you, someone knows something.

"This is an organization . . . a team of strong-willed men that have taken the city of Newark by storm. Our rules among each other are firmly set in place. We are to smash anyone and deal with each other behind closed doors. With that being said, what the fuck is going on in our city?"

Everyone said in unison that they didn't know.

"This is the shit that pisses me off. How can none of you know what's going on, and you all have ownership of one part of town. Okay, you know what . . . this right here tells me one thing. This beef is not beyond these doors. This beef is *within* these doors." Everyone sat in silence. "We all know that if I find out, this situation will be dealt with accordingly, depending on the facts. No exceptions will be taken. I have asked you all so that will be the end of it, hopefully. This meeting is over, but I need to talk to Samahd and BJ." After everyone left, BJ and Samahd moved closer to Abdule.

"What's good, Ab?"

"I should be asking you," Abdule smirked.

"I'll have it figured out soon enough."

"Listen, man. I know you and D Roc are getting into it, and I also know that his greed for what you have is what pushes him on. I really don't think he even cares too much about you killing Red anymore. Over time, his hate for you has taken over that. You need to be careful."

"I understand where you're coming from, Ab."

"Good. So how's that little lady of yours?"

"She's getting ready to pop any minute. As a matter of fact, I'm getting ready to go home right now."

"All right, then. I'll get at you later."

Michelle was at home worried about Samahd.

"Donna, did Samahd call today?"

"Nope. He said he was going to run some errands, then he was coming back. He should be here any minute. Stop worrying."

"That's easy for you to say. Your boyfriend wasn't just shot last week."

"Girl, shut the hell up and leave me alone."

"You just let me know if my man calls. I'm going in . . . Awwww, shit!"

"What's wrong?"

"I don't know but my stomach is killing

me."

"Are you serious?"

"Of course, I'm serious."

"Mama! I think Michelle's going into labor!"

Michelle's mother came flying in from the kitchen. "Are you okay, baby?"

"No, Mama! I feel like I'm dying over here."

"Come on, Donna. Help me get her in the car, and yo' ass better not bleed on my seats."

"Ma, stop playing and let's go. Donna, leave a note on the door for Samahd."

Moments after they took Michelle to the hospital, Samahd arrived. Before he got out, he sat in the car reflecting on the whole day for a moment. "This shit is getting crazy," he said to himself. "I'm going to have to kill this tall motherfucka. Fuck it. Let me get my ass in the house before Michelle tries to kill me next." He laughed and got out of the car. Immediately, he noticed the note on the door with his name on it. His eyes widened as he read it. Once he was finished he jumped in the car and burned rubber to the hospital.

Samahd got to the hospital in record time. He ran in and asked where Michelle was. The nurse notified him that she was on the third floor. Once he had the information, he bypassed the elevator and ran up the stairs. All he could hear was Michelle yelling from the room directly next to the stairs. He bolted through the door just as Michelle was pushing the baby's head out.

"Come here, baby," Michelle panted. "Hold my hand." Samahd grabbed her hand as she continued to push their son into the world.

16
THE ADDICTION

Samahd and Michelle's family stood around her to keep her calm.

"I can't believe the doctor said my baby's addicted to heroin," Michelle sobbed.

"Baby, just calm down," Samahd consoled her. "The doctor will be back to explain more in a few." At the close of that statement, the doctor walked back into the room.

"Hello, again," the doctor greeted everyone. "May I speak to you in private, Michelle?"

"Yes, sir. This is my son's father."

Donna and her mother stepped out of the room.

"Michelle, I have bad news. Your son has heroin in his bloodstream, which is making him refuse his milk. I'm sure you're not surprised, considering that you have been using heroin during your pregnancy."

"Yeah, Doc, but I didn't think it would make my baby sick."

"What did you think was going to happen when you were putting powder up your nose?"

"Hold on, Doc," Samahd interrupted. "You're out of line. This is my fiancée, and she's made a mistake. Our only concern is our son and how we can make him healthy enough to take him home."

"He will have to stay here until he kicks his habit."

"How long are we talking?"

"A month or maybe more, depending on how bad of a habit he has. You will be released tomorrow, Michelle. I highly suggest you begin detox, especially if you're going to breast-feed. Also, I apologize for stepping out of line. Sometimes these situations get to me. I understand that people make mistakes. Thank you for explaining."

"Thank you, Doc."

"I'll tell your mother and sister they can come back in now. Take care, young lady."

As Michelle got ready to leave the hospital the next day, she was terribly hurt because she had to leave a piece of her behind. Samahd pulled the car out front as the nurse wheeled Michelle to the curb. He got out and helped her in the car.

"Cheer up, baby. I know you didn't mean to hurt little Kareem."

"No, I didn't, Samahd, but that's the point. I should have listened to you before."

"I know, baby, but now is not the time to act like this. We have to deal with this situation and be strong for Kareem."

"You're right. I'm coming up here every day until it's time to take him home."

"That's cool with me, now let's go. I got a surprise for you."

Samahd and Michelle drove off. Before long he was pulling in front of his mother's house.

"Why are you stopping here?"

"Stop asking questions and come on."

Samahd walked past his mother's door and upstairs to the second floor. He handed Michelle a key. "Here, open the door."

When Michelle opened the door, she was speechless. The kitchen was beautiful with all new furniture and fixtures. "Go inside. My mother was nice enough to give me the second floor now that I have a son coming home soon."

"This is the best thing anybody has done for me. I love it." Michelle walked around in awe of their new home.

"I'm glad you like it. All you have to do is bring your clothes. My mother decorated the baby's room."

"Where's your mother? I want to thank her."

"You can catch up with her later. I need to go and find BJ."

BJ stood at Ruth's house peeking out of the window. When Samahd and Michelle arrived, he told everyone to get ready. Samahd used his key and opened the door.

"Why the fuck is it so dark in here?" Samahd pretended to complain as he turned on the lights.

"Surprise!" all of Samahd's friends yelled.

"Oh my God!" Michelle squealed in surprise. "You guys are too much."

"Here you go," Ruth said as she gave her a piece of cake. "Take this, sit down, and open all the presents we bought for you and the baby."

"Take good care of her, Ruth. I need to step outside and talk to BJ."

"You know she's in good hands."

"I know she is. Come on, BJ."

Samahd and BJ walked outside and sat on the porch to talk about the past events and the money. "How's everything looking?"

"I really think it's time to see Ab. We might, and I do stress the word *might*, have one key left."

"We went through those last 40 already?"

"This new team is stronger than ever. Ya boy John got a killer squad."

"What do you mean?"

"Them little dudes can sell just as much dope as we can . . . blow for blow."

"That's perfect. I'm thinking about askin' Ab for a bigger shipment."

"Are you serious? If you get a load bigger than the one we're already getting, we'll be moving just as much as Ab." Samahd smiled at his general. "Cuzz, you crazy."

"For real, though, I've gotta get more because it's getting ready to get cold, and I'm gettin' ready to hit the block."

"For what when you don't need to?"

"So much has happened, I need to get back in my mode."

"I can feel that."

"Good, because you'll be puttin' in more hours, too."

"Come on, man. Don't start that shit."

"We have to tighten up."

"Anyway . . . what's up with D Roc? I'm ready to off his ass."

"Just be easy for now. The time will come."

"Good, because I'm ready."

"In the meantime, I need to get with Ab. Now, let's go back inside so I can check on my baby."

17
TIME TO FOCUS

The afternoon found D Roc and Taywan on Prince Street watching the flow of traffic.

"Look at all this bread, Roc. This shit is pumping today."

"I see that, but the rest of our blocks aren't moving like this one. That's a problem. Look at New Community. It's slowed way down. That used to be my most profitable block. When I put you in charge, I thought that you would run them both the same, yet I still only have one main block. As a matter of fact, you know what, Tay?"

"What's that, Roc?"

"I want you to take your best runners and put them in New Community first thing in the morning. I want you out there all this week watching over everything. Your other people can run this block because everyone knows them."

"Consider it done."

"Good . . . Now what's up for tonight? Where's the party?"

"There's a party at the Eleganza tonight."

"Let's ride out then."

Samahd sat on Elizabeth Avenue talking to Abdule.

"What's up, old man?" Samahd clowned.

"I'll show you old." Abdule threw a couple of jabs at Samahd.

"You better slow down before you have a heart attack."

"Boy, you crazy. What's up?"

"How's shit movin'?"

"You know how we do it . . . steady movement."

"I can dig that, but I need to get straight before the month's out."

"No problem. You know I got you." Abdule noticed how Samahd's expression had changed. "What's up, Samahd? You look like something's bothering you."

"Like what?"

"Come on, man. Talk to ya boy."

"Well, you know Michelle had the baby about three days ago."

"Word! That's great."

"I know, but it's just that Michelle was gettin' high while she was pregnant."

"Say no more. I already know where this is going. Is your son okay?"

"Yeah, but he has to stay in the hospital for a while."

"That's not too bad. I've been through it before so I can tell you from experience, it'll be okay. This calls for a celebration."

"Hold on, Ab. There's one more thing. I

need more than my usual 40 joints."

"Damn, Samahd. How many are you talking?"

"I was thinking I could get maybe 20 more."

"Do you think you can handle that?"

"I really need more, but that'll do."

"Where does the sudden income come from?"

"I just came across a couple of true soldiers."

"You've always been one lucky dude."

"I guess Allah does watch over us all."

"He truly does, Samahd. Don't worry about your order. I'll have young blood bring it to you or BJ today."

"That's perfect."

"Good. Now take a ride with me."

"Where to?"

"Don't ask questions; Just ride." The two Kings jumped in Abdule's Porsche and rode off.

Samahd sat looking out the window as Abdule moved through the streets blowing the horn every so often paying his respects as people waved. He had respect from all sides as Samahd only had that much respect on one side.

"Do you see all the respect I get as I ride

through every hood, Samahd?"

"I can see that."

"Okay . . . This is what I want to show you. You don't need this in your life. You don't want to have to watch everyone. It's a given that certain people are going to know you, but you have to just stay low. If for nothing else, do it for my sake."

"Damn, Ab, that's real. I really appreciate this."

"Thanks, Samahd, but I don't want you to just *hear* me, I want you to *listen*. Take heed to what I'm trying to teach you. If you think you got problems with D Roc now, it'll be ten times worse down the line. I have to keep my eyes open for everyone—even people from out of town. They come at me from all angles. I don't want this for you. When I'm done, you'll be the next in line."

"Why are you telling me this?"

"I'm getting old, and you're getting strong. I can see in you the same thing I saw in myself a few years back. I want you to think about everything I've said to you and use it to study and learn your surroundings."

"I will, Ab. I give you my word on that, and always know that I'm here for you. I will not, and I reiterate, *not* let anyone touch you without death."

"I know. Now let's go and celebrate the birth of your son. I hear the Eleganza is jumping off tonight."

"The El it is."

John sat on Mapes in the old movie theater parking lot watching the flow of traffic.

"Tim!" John called. "Come here for a minute."

"What's up, John?"

"Come over here and look out there. Tell me what you see."

"People hustling, running back and forth."

"Now tell me what's wrong with this picture."

"I don't know. What?"

"You just said it. Everyone is running wild."

"I can see that."

"Don't you think things would be a little better if they were a little more organized?"

"I guess so."

"Organized crime is the best and most kept, but on the flip side, it's the most dangerous. For example, look at Samahd and BJ. They're already involved in organized crime, yet the block is not. We need to make it better, and in return, BJ and Samahd will be happy. Samahd is already one of the Four Kings of Newark, and everyone knows this."

"I didn't," Tim replied with surprise.

"Well, now you do. That's why people are trying to beef with us. Even though we're young in the game, we're the first line of defense. We need to get all the underbosses from our team and have a meeting."

"We can do that, so what do you have in mind?"

"I got a plan for this block to bring in twice the money with minimum risk. Now I need you to gather everyone that has runners."

"I'm on it."

BJ was sitting on Mapes when he noticed Donna pulling up in Michelle's car.

"What's up, Donna?" BJ greeted.

"Hi, BJ. What you been up to?"

"I'm just tryna stay outta trouble."

"That's good. Keep it up."

"You're a comedian now," BJ laughed.

"I'm for real."

"How about you help me stay outta trouble."

"What can I do to help you with that?"

"Spend a couple of hours with me."

"And do what? I'm not trying to be one of your hoes. I'm too good for that."

"I know you are, and I'm not asking you to be my ho. I want to spend some time with you."

"Well, I came to bring Michelle's car back. Let me take her the keys and I'll be right back." Donna walked upstairs and gave Michelle her keys. The two sisters had a short conversation, then Donna returned to link back up with BJ.

When she got to the street, he wasn't there. In a few moments, BJ honked the horn as he pulled up.

"Come on," BJ called from the car.

"Where we going?"

"We're going to New York so I can take you shopping."

"Now you're speakin' my language," Donna smiled. She hopped in the car as BJ handed her a nice bundle.

"Is this how you bag all your bitches? You get 'em high and take 'em shopping?"

"Hell, nah. It's just that ever since the last time we hung out, I've been waiting for this. Now I'm going to take advantage of the situation and treat you like I should've from the beginning."

"I never knew you thought of me after

that night."

"Now you know. Now take one of these and bust it open."

"Okay, Big Daddy."

"Now *that's* how I like it."

Later on that evening, Samahd made his way home to get dressed to celebrate his son with Abdule. He noticed John sitting in the old parking lot when he got out of the car. He walked over to talk to him. When John saw Samahd, he jumped up and met him halfway. Samahd greeted John with a tight embrace.

"You good?" Samahd asked.

"Everything is cool."

"That's good, because I need to talk to you about something."

"What's up?"

"I'm moving your rank up. You're no longer a soldier. Now you're a knight."

"I appreciate that."

"Good, because now you have more responsibility. I'm giving you a whole brick today, and you're gonna have to make your own bundles. I'll take care of bagging everything, and you just take it from there."

"Say no more . . . I'm on it."

"Did Abdul come by Ruth's today?"

"Yeah. He left about 30 minutes ago."

"All right. I'm going in the house and get dressed to go out. I'll see you before I leave. Is Michelle in the house?"

"I don't know. I haven't seen her all day. If she's not there, then she's probably at the hospital."

"Okay."

18
BABY K

Samahd walked into the hospital with such an undeniable presence.

"May I help you?" The nurse behind the desk asked.

"Yes, you can. I'm looking for the children's ward. I'm here to visit my son."

"Okay. Take a left to the elevator and go to the second floor." The nurse could barely speak as she admired Samahd's appearance.

"Thank you, young lady. You have a nice day."

Samahd made his way upstairs and stepped off of the elevator when he was met by another woman.

"Can I help you?"

"I'm looking for Kareem Hicks."

"Let me check." The nurse looked on her clipboard. "Go to Room 236 and you should see his name on one of the incubators."

"Thank you."

When Samahd made it to the room, he saw Michelle standing in the window. He snuck up behind her and placed a soft kiss on her neck. Michelle turned around with anger until she realized that it was Samahd.

"Hey, baby. You scared me. What are you doing up here?"

"I can't come see my son?"

"Of course, you can come see your son. I

just thought you were busy, that's all."

"I'll never be too busy to check on the world's two most important to me."

"I'm glad you feel that way."

"So how's Kareem?"

"The doctor said he's so strong."

Looking down at his son, Samahd said, "That's right. Fight so you can come home with Daddy and Mommy." A tear fell from the Samahd's eye. Michelle put her arms around him.

"The doctor said if he continues like this, then we should be able to take him home in a couple of weeks."

"That's great!" The young couple stood looking down at their son. "Okay, baby. I gotta go."

"That's cool. I'll see you at home."

After a couple of hours of shopping in New York, BJ and Donna were sitting down to dinner.

"Thank you for showing me a great time," Donna expressed.

"It's all good. I just wanted to show you that I can be a nice guy sometimes. I don't treat all women the same. My thing is that I haven't found a woman really worth me giving a damn about. These chicks out here are only checkin' for me because of who I am and what I represent."

"So why me?"

"Because I never got the chance to show you what I was really about. Before I knew it, we kicked it, and then you were with Sadeek. Now it's time for a real man to show you a good time."

"I'm already having a good time."

BJ and Donna continued to converse over dinner. As they talked, they found out that they had a lot in common. Once they finished. They left.

Samahd came roaring down Meeker on his way to meet Abdule. Al Green was in the air, and he was feeling better than ever. He stopped on Elizabeth Avenue and hopped in the car with Abdule.

"*That's* the Samahd I'm used to seeing," Abdule laughed as he pulled off. "You look a hellavah lot better than you did earlier."

"I just left the hospital. Little man is doing good. Doc said we should be able to bring him home in a couple of weeks."

"*That's* what's up. It's still early so let's stop at Roland's for a minute."

The two Kings blazed down the street. When they got to Roland's, Samahd saw Smiley sitting in front of the Chinese store across the street. He told Abdule that he needed to talk to him and that he'd meet him inside.

"What's up, Smiley?"

"I'm coolin', big homie," Smiley laughed. "Just out here chasin' this paper."

"I can dig it. I've been lookin' for you."

"What's up?"

"I need you to turn it up on Shepherd. Then I'll show you something."

"That's easy. All I have to do is stay outside. If I do that, what will you show me?"

"How to really get this paper. I'm going to tell BJ and John to keep their eyes on you. If they think you're ready for what we're about to do, then I'll be coming to see you."

"Say word? I've been waiting to join the winning team."

"Just play your position and I got you." Samahd finished his conversation and headed into Roland's.

Despite the fact that it was early, Roland's was still jumping. Abdule and Samahd walked up to the bar.

"Hey, Miss Betty," Samahd greeted with a smile.

"Hey, boy! Why you ain't came to see

me since you been outta the hospital?"

"I'm sorry, Miss Betty. Things have been crazy since I got out, but I'm here now. As a matter of fact, give everybody a round on me and keep the change."

"You're too good to me. Come here and gimme a hug."

Samahd and Betty embraced as he looked on proudly at all the love. As Betty hugged him, she noticed Abdule standing behind him.

"How you doing, Abdule?"

"I'm doing good, and you?"

"Good now that I've seen my baby. Samahd's like a son to me."

"I did not know that."

"Now you know."

"If this is your first time seeing Miss Betty," Abdule grinned, "then she doesn't know."

"Know what, Samahd?"

"You really tryna get me shot tonight!" Samahd laughed. "I had my son a couple of days ago."

"You just treat me so bad, Samahd."

"Don't act like that. You know I was going to tell you the first chance I got."

"I'll deal with you later. Let me serve these aggravating-ass people."

John sat in the middle of Ruth's living room calling the meeting to order. In attendance were Tranel, Tim, G Boss, Sadeek, as well as him.

"All right, fellas," John began, "I need you to pay attention and listen to what I'm getting ready to say. We're all getting good money, yet we don't have any kind of organization among ourselves. Samahd and BJ are getting ready to make big moves. Earlier today, Samahd made me a knight. I am the highest level of defense. With this power I'm going to strengthen our block better than ever.

"The first thing we have to do is find more runners to take turns on shifts. We need people on the roofs of Bergen and Mapes, Shepherd and Lehigh. That way, we can be in the middle of the block and see from all angles. Any questions about what we're trying to accomplish?"

"No!" everyone replied in unison.

"I like it," Tranel said.

"Good, because you and I are going to be in charge of this new operation."

"You know I'm with it."

"Then it's all settled. You all know your positions and what you're supposed to do. Let's go get some drinks on me." The meeting adjourned, and the men left.

BJ and Donna walked hand in hand out of the Statue of Liberty.

"How was that?" BJ asked as he pulled Donna closer and put his arm around her.

"I loved it, BJ. I never knew your idea of having a good time would be looking at the skyline of New York."

"What are you trying to say?"

"That you just act hard, but deep down inside, you have a gentle side."

"All men have a gentle side. We just don't know how to find it sometimes."

"I'm glad you found yours. You have truly showed me the best time ever. What's the catch?"

"There's no catch. I just want to spend time with you."

"I understand that, but why?"

"Because I really like you."

Samahd and Abdule pulled up to the El and got out. All eyes were on them as Abdule gave the valet his keys wrapped in a hundred dollar bill. Once spotted, women began to call Abdule's name from every direction. When they walked in the club, the DJ gave them a shout-out and a congrats to Samahd on the birth of his son. They slid through the crowd to the bar. Samahd noticed two females staring at him and Abdule and pointed them out to him. Abdule told the bartender to send the girls an expensive bottle of champagne as he and Samahd started toward the women. They introduced themselves.

"Hello, ladies. I'm Abdule, and this is my right-hand man, Samahd. And you are?"

"I'm Vicky, and this is Stacey."

As they exchanged pleasantries, the bartender arrived with the champagne and four glasses. "Who is this from?"

"The gentlemen you're speaking with," the bartender replied.

"Thank you, sweetheart, I can take it from here." Abdule grabbed the bottle and poured the champagne.

19

MAKE IT A NIGHT

D Roc and Taywan arrived at the El in a stretch Cadillac limousine. The chauffeur opened the door for them to step out and walk into the club. Just as he did with Abdule and Samahd, the DJ shouted out D Roc and Taywan. Samahd perked up when he heard D Roc's name.

"Did you hear that?" Samahd said to Abdule.

"Yeah, I heard it. Just ease back and see if they notice us."

"In the meantime, I'll keep my eyes on them."

"What are you ladies getting into later on tonight?"

"That's up to you," Vicky smiled. "But I like where I'm at right now."

"Where you from?"

"I'm from North Carolina, and Stacey's from Virginia. We're students at Montclair University."

"Oh, okay. I see we have us a couple of Southern belles. I like that." Abdule and Vicky continued to talk. Stacey made her way to the dance floor while Samahd sat with his eyes locked on D Roc and Taywan. Vicky noticed that Samahd looked upset and asked him what was wrong.

"Are you okay, Samahd?" she asked.

"I'm cool . . . just keeping my eye on a couple of my friends across the room."

"It doesn't look like they're good friends the way you're staring at them."

"I'm glad you noticed that. You're a smart girl."

"Thanks for the compliment, but I have four brothers. It's kinda easy to tell when they're upset."

"I'll be back, Ab. I'm going to speak to our friends." Samahd got up to walk over to D Roc and Taywan.

"Samahd," Abdule called, "be cool."

"I'm cool."

D Roc and Taywan were at the bar without a care in the world.

"Bartender!" Taywan called over the music. "Free rounds for everybody. Make sure everyone gets a drink on Tay."

Roc and Tay continued to dance to the music until Roc felt someone tap him on the shoulder. Thinking it was a female, D Roc tried to turn around as smooth as he could. To his surprise, it was Samahd.

"What's good?" D Roc greeted with a phony smile.

"I'm good. What's up with you?"

"I'm just out with Tay."

Turning around and noticing Samahd,

Tay said, "What's up, Big Dog?" then turned back to the bartender. "Let me get a double shot for my man right here."

"Coming right up."

"Let me cut right through the bullshit," Samahd began looking D Roc straight in the eyes. "You ain't fooling nobody."

"What are you talking about?"

"I know what you tried to do. I ain't no fuckin' dummy. You might not have done it yourself, but you had something to do with it. Next time you need to hire some worthy soldiers to come at me."

"Hold on, Samahd. Why would you come at me like that? I had nothing to do with what happened to you. I'm tryna find the people responsible for it my self."

"I hear that bullshit you talkin', but let me tell you something. The next time anything points in your direction, I'm going to personally murder your ass the same fuckin' night."

"Why so hostile? I understand your anger, but we're supposed to be on the same team."

"That's what I thought, too. Obviously I was wrong. Me and Ab are sitting over there. I didn't want to say what I had to say in front of him. Come pay your respects."

D Roc sat there for a moment taking in what Samahd had just said to him.

"Did you hear how Samahd was talking to me?" D Roc asked.

"Hell, yeah. I heard every word. I feel like he said it loud enough for me to hear."

"I believe you might be right. I told you to come correct or not at all. Now I really have to keep my eyes on that motherfucka. Order four bottles and have them send them over to the tables. When you finish, come over to the table."

D Roc walked to the table with as much style as he could muster. "What's good, Ab?"

"How you, Roc?"

"Me and Taywan just out here tryna have some fun."

"That's cool. I take it you didn't see Samahd sitting over here."

"Nah, Ab. I didn't know either of you were here."

"Thank Allah because for a minute my feelings were about to be hurt."

"Never that. It's never anything like that."

"That shows me that you're becoming too comfortable for your own good. I don't walk into any place without observing my surroundings."

"You're right. I should know better."

"You need to get your shit together," Samahd laughed.

"Don't be so hard on your teammate," Abdule joked. "You're both on the same team. Right, D Roc?"

"Of course, Ab." The bartender arrived with the drinks for the group. Samahd handed her a hundred dollar bill.

"Can I get anyone anything else?" she asked as she blushed while looking at Samahd.

"No, bitch . . . bye," Vicky said as she rolled her eyes.

"Calm down," Abdule said trying to sooth Vicky.

"I just don't like disrespectful women."

"How did she disrespect you? She was talking to Samahd."

"I know, but my girl is tryna get at him."

Stacey walked back to the group and sat down as close as she could to Samahd.

"You okay?" she asked, kissing him on the cheek.

"I'm good."

"What's wrong with you, Vicky?"

"I'm all right. These thirsty broads out here are just pissin' me off."

"Just don't get started in here. You know how you are."

"I'm cool."

"Good," Abdule interrupted. "Now, let's enjoy the night."

"You a rude nigga," D Roc jokingly said to Abdule. "You're not going to introduce me to the lovely ladies?"

"This is Vicky and Stacey. They go to Montclair."

"Where your friends at?"

"We don't have friends at school. That's why we party by ourselves. Those chicks from school don't like us cuz we're from down South."

"I can understand that." D Roc turned back to Abdule. "What brings you and Samahd to this part of town?"

"We're out celebrating the birth of Samahd's son."

The Kings and the ladies sat and enjoyed the night. Before long, D Roc and Taywan excused themselves to go find their own ladies. Samahd and Abdule sat for a little while longer, then they prepared themselves to leave.

"You rolling with us, Samahd?" Abdule asked as he downed the last drop of champagne in his glass.

"I guess I'll ride since it's still early."

Abdule instructed the girls to go get their car and they'd meet them outside. "Yo, Ab . . .

go ahead to the car. I'm going to say my good-byes to D Roc and Taywan."

"Remember what I told you. Be cool."

"I got you." Samahd found D Roc on the dance floor and tapped him on the shoulder again. "Let me kick it with you for a minute before I leave."

"What's up?"

"Look here, Cuz. I want you to remember what I told you because I meant every word of it."

"I can dig it, but let me tell you something. If I come at you . . . I won't miss. Make sure *you* remember *that*."

"Consider it well understood," Samahd smiled as he walked off.

20

A Bond

BJ led Donna into a suite at the Hilton.

"This room is amazing," Donna squealed. "Look at the bed and all the rose petals. We got wine and everything."

"All this is cool, but it doesn't mean as much to me as you do."

"Thank you, BJ. That means a lot to me." Donna walked over to the cart and poured two glasses of wine. "Come sit down over here." When BJ got closer, she handed him a glass of wine and began to massage his neck.

"That feels good," BJ replied as he downed his drink.

"Good . . . now lie back on the bed."

BJ obliged her request as she slid him out of his pants. After she had them off, she took his nine inches into her hand, then placed in her mouth.

Back in Newark, John, Tranel, Tim, and G Boss sat at the bar inside of Roland's. John told Miss Betty to give everyone a round on him and a bottle of Remy Martin for him and his crew.

"You know we're getting ready to change the game after we make this move on Bergen," John began. "Once we set it off, everybody else is gonna follow suit. We'll be hood legends."

"That's right," Tranel agreed.

"We gotta be strong and back down to no one. We live by the gun and die by the gun. Everybody take your guns and put them on the bar." The three others pulled their pieces out and placed them on the bar. "Now take out one bullet and put it in your glass. As I pour the liquor in, take the glass into your hands. This is our creed. As we drink, our code is bonded together. We swallow the bullet along with any fears that we might have. Strengthen us as we move all our enemies behind us. Now at the same time, we drink!!!!!"

Not too far away, Samahd and Abdule were riding in the elevator with the two ladies from the club. They led the girls to a double suite at the end of the hall. As they neared the room, Stacey noticed the expression on Samahd's face.

"What's wrong, baby?"

"I'm good . . . just thinking about my son."

"You're going to be a great father."

"Thank you for being so considerate."

"You're welcome . . . now let's make it to the bed so you can really thank me, and I can make you feel better."

"All right, you two," Abdule laughed. "Take it inside."

"I know you ain't talkin'. You been all over Vicky from the front door to here."

"That's not nice," Vicky laughed. "As a matter of fact, come here." Samahd walked toward Vicky. Before he could get there good, she shoved her tongue down his throat.

"Now *that's* what I'm talkin' about," Abdule laughed.

"We haven't shown you anything yet," Vicky grinned. "Come here, Stacey." Stacey walked over, dropped to her knees and wrapped her lips around Samahd's dick while Vicky was still kissing him. "Don't think you're off the hook, Ab. You come here, too."

"Yes, ma'am." Abdule dropped his pants and joined the party. Vicky unlocked from Samahd's lips and put them on Abdule's dick.

Stacey released Samahd and crawled over to the couch. Samahd watched as she got there and positioned herself for him to take her from behind. "Come take me, Big Daddy." When Samahd got there he smacked her left ass cheek, then slid inside of her. Stacey let out a loud scream. Abdule and Vicky made it to their room with her legs wrapped around him and him still inside of her. He continued to lift her up and down as she reached her climax. Once finished, Samahd and Abdule pulled the old switcheroo and continued through the night.

***

Michelle woke up from a dream of Kareem in Weequahic Park playing with Samahd when she heard the door open.

"Is that you, Samahd?" Michelle called.

"Yeah, it's me."

"How was your night?"

"It was all right. Me and Ab went to the El and had some drinks."

"Sounds like you had a good time."

"It was cool."

"Now come to bed. I want you to hold me."

"Okay, baby. Let me hop in the shower first."

21

I'M BACK

Samahd woke up the next morning and got dressed.

"Where you going?" Michelle asked as she lay in bed.

"I got a bunch of stuff to put together so I have to round everybody up."

"Can't someone else do that?"

"The only one that can do that is BJ, but I haven't heard from him since yesterday."

"He's with Donna somewhere."

"Your sister Donna?"

"Yeah. If you recall, we all started out together."

"I know, but I didn't think she liked BJ like that."

"She liked him; she just didn't like the way he was with so many different women."

"That doesn't surprise me," Samahd chuckled. "Anyway . . . I gotta go. I'll be back as soon as I can take care of everything."

"I love you, Samahd."

"I love you, too."

At Ruth's house, John was inside sitting on the couch thinking about the night before. *I need to get my ass up and get outside*, he thought to himself. At the passing of that thought, he heard keys in the door. Thinking it was BJ, he hopped up and went to open the door like he was walking out. It was Samahd.

"What's up, Samahd," he greeted.

"I'm good. You haven't been outside yet?"

"Not yet. I was just waking up. My bad."

"I'm glad you told the truth, cuz there's some people outside looking for you."

"I actually thought you were BJ. You know how he is about being outside for the first shift."

"I know. I made him that way."

"Thanks for lettin' me slide."

"Normally I wouldn't, but me and BJ been slippin' too. We as leaders have to lead by example. With that being said, we all have to tighten up. I'm tryna recover from a wild-ass night fuckin' wit' Ab."

"Tell me about it. Me and the fellas got it in, too."

"Before you hit the block, I need to talk to you on a personal level."

"What's up?"

"You know I love your sister, and you know how this life is. Sometimes I cut out and do a li'l something on the side. The thing that bothers me is that it seems like she always knows when I do."

"Listen, Samahd. You got a lot of money,

and women are gonna throw themselves at you. Even though you got a girl and a child, you're still young. You're on track more than most. One day you'll be able to give up the fast life and marry my sister. I'm not taking sides, but I do know you're a good person."

"Look at you tryna be all philosophical and shit," Samahd laughed. "I just wanted to bring it to you before somebody else did."

"We good, Samahd."

"No doubt. Now let's get down to business. We got a lot of shit to do today. The first thing I need you to do is round up the girls and get them back here ASAP. Then I need you to go to the store and get the cut, bags, rubber bands, and all the newspapers you can find. Come straight back here. I don't want you riding around or being followed back here with all that stuff. Don't try to buy everything from one store. Go to a different store for each item."

"Got it."

BJ dropped Donna off at home and pulled up on Mapes early that morning. When he pulled up at Ruth's, John was coming out of the house.

"Where you going?" BJ asked.

"I'm going to get the girls and the bags."

"Word? Who told you to do that?"

"Samahd."

"Where is he?"

"He's in the house going over the package."

"Bet."

BJ walked in the house and heard Samahd in the back room. He poked his head in the room. "What's good?"

"Where you been, man?"

"I did some crazy shit last night, and I'm not sure if it was right or wrong."

"What do you mean?"

"I took Donna to New York and let her know how I really felt about her."

"What's the problem with that?"

"The problem is that I don't want to hurt her."

"I understand that, but do you understand that?"

"I guess so. I'll just have to get used to being with one person, that's all."

"That's going to take a lot of work," Samahd laughed. "Anyway, I have started getting everything together so we can have at least half of these bricks done today."

"Do you want the girls to stay overnight so we can get everything together?"

"I'm not sure. If we do, we have to move

this shit in two or three weeks." Samahd sat and thought for a second. "As a matter of fact, give the order. I want all the girls to do overtime. We'll pay them double, and I'm not takin' no for an answer. If they disagree, I want 'em dead because I don't trust 'em. It's time to take it to the next level. You with me?"

"From the cradle to the grave."

22
BREAKING THE RULES

An hour later, John made it back to Ruth's house as the rest of the girls were walking in the front door. When he hopped out, he saw Tranel down the street. He called to him.

"What's good, Cuz?" John greeted as he approached.

"Same shit."

"Help me grab this shit out of the car."

They grabbed everything and walked into a house full of naked women.

"I think I just walked through the gates of Heaven," Tranel laughed. "Look at that thick, light-skinned one right there."

Samahd walked into the front room to take count of the women when he noticed that one of them wasn't present.

"Where's Lisa?"

"She's with some dude from across town," one of the girls answered. "She said that she didn't need you or this shit anymore."

"What's your name?"

"My name is Yvette, and I told her she was dumb for turning her back on you when you've been so good to her this past year."

"I wonder why she's outta pocket all of a sudden."

"Dude got her head gassed up, and now she thinks she's too good to get money."

"I've known Lisa for seven years, and this past year is the best she's ever been able to take care of her kids. Enough about that. I'm sorry I haven't taken the time to get to know all of you a little better than I have. The only reason I know Lisa like that is because she was the head woman. I'd like to thank you, Yvette, for all of your information, and now you are head woman. I know John gave you girls your instructions, but let me go over it again. I need you to stay overnight so you can get all of your work done. I don't need to remind you all of what will happen if you steal from me. You all will be paid double for staying an extra couple of hours. I need you on your A game. Let's get to work."

Samahd called for John.

"What's up, Samahd?"

"What are you and Tranel doing in the back?"

"We were helping BJ get the whole bricks together to be bust down."

"Don't worry about that. I need you and Tranel to do something important for me."

"Anything you need."

"Do you remember where that chick Lisa stay at?"

"Yeah. That's the first place I went. Some nigga came to the door. I told him I needed to speak to Lisa, and he got real funny acting. I brushed it off because she came to the door right after him. I let her know what was up, and she said she was coming."

"Did you notice that she wasn't here?"

"I didn't notice."

"It's things like this that you have to be aware of when it's your turn to lead."

"That's my fault, Samahd."

"Don't stress it. I know it's hard for a young man your age to focus in a room full of butt-naked hoes." They laughed. "I want you to go to her house and burn her and her nigga up. Ain't no telling what she done told this nigga about my operation."

"I got you, my G."

"Now' grab ya boy and get it done."

In a parked car, John and Tranel sat watching Lisa's house.

"This bitch ain't came out all day," Tranel complained. "I thought we woulda had this shit done by now. It's already dark, and I ain't made no money all day."

"Fuck it. It's my call. Let's creep around back and see what room they're in."

John and Tranel eased out of the car and crept into the alley. When they peeked in, they saw Lisa and her man in the bedroom watching TV.

"This is what we're gonna do. We kick in the back door and make it look like a robbery gone bad. Kill everybody in the house except for the kids."

"What if they see our faces?"

"I got that covered. Take this flag and strap up."

John ran up on the back porch and kicked the door open. Before Lisa and her man could do anything, Tranel and John were already in the room.

"What the fuck y'all niggas want?" Lisa screamed as they rushed in the room.

"Shut the fuck up, bitch!" John barked. "Nigga, I wish you would move off that bed."

"Talk about catchin' a nigga wit' his dick in the dirt," Tranel laughed. "Now open your mouth right now." Tranel put the barrel of the gun in his mouth. "Now close it. If you open ya mouth again, I'm pullin' the trigger."

"Hold up," Lisa pleaded. "I know Samahd sent you. I'm sorry for not coming. He probably thinks I'm going to double-cross—" Before she could finish, John squeezed one right between her eyes.

"Baby!" Lisa's boyfriend mumbled with the barrel in his mouth.

"I told you not to open your mouth again," Tranel replied as he pulled the trigger.

"Check on the kids," John commanded. Tranel opened the door and saw two kids hugging each other, trembling in fear.

"When we leave, call the police. Here's some money. Put it in your pockets and use what you need."

John walked in the room.

"Come on. Let's go."

Back on Mapes, Samahd sat in his GTO in the old parking lot watching his surroundings. He noticed that things were a lot different than when he used to be out there hustling his own product. "This whole block is changing right before my eyes. I need to start coming out again to keep up with what's going on." G Boss walked by and noticed Samahd sitting in the car.

"What the hell you doin' sittin' out here by yourself?" G asked as he approached the car.

"I'm just puttin' time in on the block. You ain't got no work."

"I know, and that's my fault. Let's go grab some smoke from Smiley and we'll go to Ruth's house so I can get you something to hold you over until everything's ready. And just because you my man, you can keep the whole thing."

"Damn, I need that. Good looking out."

"You know I take care of my team."

Samahd and G Boss walked around the corner to Shepherd and Bergen to find Smiley.

BJ stood in Ruth's house on the phone talking to Donna.

"What's up?" BJ asked.

"Nothing but missing you. When are we going to spend some more time together?"

"Right now I have to finish things up over here. After I'm done, we can get together and do something. If I don't finish up tonight, I promise we'll do something tomorrow."

"Okay. I guess I'll talk to you later."

"Hold on, Donna. Before you hang up, I just wanted to tell you that I had the time of my life with you. There has never been a woman that I have felt closer to than you. As soon as I get through here, I'll call you."

As Samahd, G Boss, and Smiley sat in the parking lot smoking, Samahd noticed the quality of weed and asked Smiley about it.

"I got it from a Jamaican cat from across town. Tim put me on to him."

"This shit can make us some money out here."

"I can plug you in if you need me to."

"I'll let you know."

They continued to chop it up. Tranel and John noticed them in the parking lot and pulled in.

"I know y'all ain't out here blowin' some of Newark's finest without ya boy," Tranel laughed as he hopped out of the car. "Let me hit that, Samahd."

"You got some information for me?"

"Everything's done."

"My man," Samahd smiled as he passed the smoke to Tranel.

"Let me tell you about your boy right here," John began as he laughed. "This crazy-ass nigga shot dude in the mouth. That ain't the funny part though. Then he had the nerve to say 'I told you so' to a dead man. I wanted to fall out laughing."

"Damn, Tranel," Smiley began. "I didn't know you put it down like that."

"When it's time to put in work, it's time to put in work. Don't worry; you'll get your turn."

"He's right," Samahd added. "Don't forget what I told you not too long ago." Samahd took one more pull of the blunt and handed it to G Boss. "I'm going to check on my girl. John, go see how BJ's coming along. Get everybody ready for tomorrow because even I'll be on the block."

23
THE NEW WAY

Samahd walked in the house and noticed Michelle in the shower. He quickly took off his clothes and went into the bathroom. Michelle heard the door open and pulled the shower curtain back.

"Hey, baby," she greeted. "I'm glad you came in the house early tonight."

"I had to take into consideration that you wouldn't stand for me coming home late every night."

"You got that right, young man. Now come in here."

"Damn, Michelle! You tryna burn all the skin off my body?"

"Stop whining. You're a tough guy, but you can't take a little hot water?"

Back at Ruth's house, BJ sat in the back room pushing the girls.

"Come on, ladies. I know y'all tired. I'm tired, too. We got 20 keys left, and then you can go. Come here for a minute, Yvette. Let me talk to you."

"Okay, BJ. Let me go get Ruth to watch over the girls." Yvette walked into the kitchen and found Ruth. "Excuse me, Ruth."

"Yes, baby."

"Can you watch the girls while I go and see what BJ wants?"

"Where did he go?"

"He walked into the front bedroom when I came to find you."

"I got you. Just don't be up there too long, if you catch my drift." Ruth smirked at Yvette.

"I get your drift. Give me about 30 minutes tops."

"I got you. You just don't forget about me later on."

"I won't. Believe me."

Yvette walked into the room and found BJ sitting on the bed rubbing his temples. "What's wrong, BJ?"

"Damn," BJ replied as she startled him. "I didn't hear you come in. I'm good. How you dealing with your new position?"

"Some girls are jealous, but besides that, everything's okay."

"That's good. Now I need you to do me a personal favor."

"Anything for you, BJ."

"Come suck this thing right here. I need to let out some tension."

"Is that all you need? I can handle that for you."

From there, a simple blow job turned into

a hot sex session. BJ bent Yvette over the bed and gave her all he had to offer.

John woke up early the next morning and drove straight to the block. When he pulled up to Ruth's house, everybody was sitting on the porch. The time on his watch displayed 5:30 A.M.

"That's what I'm talkin' about," John approved as he stepped on the porch. "What's good, fellas?"

"We sittin' here waitin' on you," Tim replied. "We ready to hit the block runnin'."

"Bet. Me and Tranel will get our packs and start everyone out. Tim and G Boss, you start your packs first. I'll take the roof, and Tranel will take the Backstreet. Let's get this show on the road."

John and Tranel walked into the house and straight to the back. "Where you at, BJ?"

"I'm in the back," BJ responded. Tim and Tranel walked in the back room and found BJ standing over the bundles putting them all together. "I see you gettin' used to all this naked pussy walkin' around here."

"Not quite yet. I'm just focused on something else this morning."

"That's what I like to hear. You know

Samahd told me to give you a whole key, right?"

"Yeah. He told me that a couple of days ago."

"Good, because I'm givin' Tranel one, too."

"I like the sound of that," John smiled.

"Me and Samahd will be on the block all week. Make sure you keep your shit together."

"Don't even worry about the block. You and Samahd are gonna see something special."

"Don't talk about it, be about it," BJ laughed. "Take these. There should be about 400 there. Take the extras. You both are responsible for $30,000 a piece."

"I'll make sure you get everything."

"All right. Now go put that shit somewhere before the police start their shift."

Later on that morning, Samahd woke up to the sun shining in the window. He felt energized and was ready to hit the block. As he moved around getting dressed, he heard a horn outside. When he peeked out the window, he saw that it was Abdule. He threw on his robe and slippers and walked outside. When he got to the car, he noticed Vicky sitting in the passenger's seat.

"What's up, Ab?" he greeted.

"I was just dropping by to see if you wanted to go grab something to eat before you hit the streets for the day."

"I appreciate that, but I'm good. I have to play it close to the house for a while. At least until Kareem comes home from the hospital. What's up with you and Vicky?"

"We've been together since yesterday. This is my new baby. I told you I liked her style." Vicky smiled as Abdule looked at her. "Anyway . . . What the fuck is going on out here? When I came through I saw lookouts on the roof, hustlers in the middle of the block, and another lookout right there on the corner." Samahd looked up the block and saw Tranel standing on the corner. Tranel gave him a nod and continued to look back and forth.

"You know I got all that extra. I told the homies they had to tighten it up around here."

"Looks like they came up with a solid plan. I'll holla at you later."

Michelle was in the kitchen cooking breakfast when Samahd walked back in. Samahd walked into the bedroom to get dressed, then came back into the kitchen to eat. Michelle was putting his food on the table when he walked in.

"Thank you, baby. What are your plans

for the day?"

"Other than going to the hospital, I don't have anything planned."

"Why don't you take a little time for yourself? Go shopping or something."

"I don't know, Samahd."

"Come on, baby. You can go out and buy some things for you and Kareem."

"I just might do that."

"Good. I'm going out to check on the homies for a while."

"Okay, baby. I'm going to get dressed. If you're gone before I get ready, I'll see you later."

When Samahd finished eating he grabbed his keys and his piece and headed for the block. As soon as he walked outside he ran into G Boss in the middle of the block.

On the corner of Bergen and Mapes, John was posted on one of the rooftops. As he watched over the block, he noticed Samahd walking down the street. He put his joint out and jumped down to greet his big hommie.

"What's going on, John? What you up to?"

"I'm on lookout right now," John replied as he pointed to the roof he'd just come from.

"Okay . . . I see you. How's everything moving today?"

"This might be one of the best days this block has seen, and I know it's seen some good days."

"What makes you so sure?" Samahd laughed.

"We moved more product this morning than we have in two days. I don't know what it is about this batch, but it's been jumping like crazy. It also has a lot to do with how we got the block running now."

"How do you have it runnin'?"

"Let's walk across the street so you can see the whole picture."

They walked across the street. "If you look in the middle of the block, you got Tim on one side and G Boss on the other. All they have to do is collect and give the work to the runners. Tranel is on the Backstreet lookin' for cops that way, and I'm up there lookin' for 'em."

"How's the system working?"

"I told you . . . Today is the best day ever. Between me and Tranel, we had about 400 bricks this morning. We might have about 300 now and the morning's not over yet."

"That ain't too bad at all. Keep it up. Where's BJ?"

"He's at Ruth's house tryna get some sleep. He was up all night making sure shit got done."

When Samahd walked into Ruth's house, BJ was asleep on the couch. All of the girls were gone except for Yvette. She and Ruth were in the back wrapping all the bags into bundles and bricking them up with five bundles to a brick. Samahd walked in and saw them hard at work.

"Hey, girls. How's everything going?"

"We're almost finished," Ruth replied.

"How long has BJ been asleep?"

"About two or three hours. I know he's tired. He put almost 6,000 bricks together on his own. We took over from there."

"I appreciate it, and thank you, Yvette, because I know you could've left when the rest of the girls left."

"Don't mention it, Samahd. I wouldn't think of leaving Ms. Ruth and BJ to do all this work."

"That's the type of attitude I need around here. How much did BJ give the girls?"

"I think he gave them $1,500 a piece."

"Then I guess you deserve $3,000 then, huh?"

"That would be nice," Yvette smiled.

"It's about time you start appreciating hard work," Ruth laughed.

"You be quiet. I'll deal with you later."

"You know you love me."

"Yes, I do. Anyway, back to you, Yvette. You're a great worker, and I would like for you to think about staying with us. All I ask is that you keep your respect and loyalty for me, my team, and my family."

"I've already chosen, Samahd. I'm with you."

"Welcome to the family. Now that you're in . . . you know that Lisa's out . . . for good. She wasn't loyal to the team, nor was she faithful with our information."

"You did what you had to do."

During the conversation, the phone rang. It was Donna calling for BJ. Ruth went into the front room and woke him up. BJ jumped up to grab the phone.

"Hey, baby."

"Hey, baby, my ass. I thought you promised to call me this morning."

"I know, baby, but I was up all night. I just fell asleep about an hour ago."

"It's okay. I'm just joking. I was just calling to see what you had planned before I started running around for the day."

"Where are you thinking about going?"

"Michelle is leaving the hospital, and she asked me if I wanted to go to the mall."

"Go ahead with your sister. That'll give

me time to get things situated on this end. Come through the block and check me out later."

"Okay, baby."

24
IT'S REAL

Back on Mapes and Bergen, John was on the roof. He noticed an unfamiliar black Oldsmobile drive around the block twice without stopping. It looked suspicious, so he jumped down to let the rest of the team know what was going on. The first person he saw was Tim.

"Have you seen that black Oldsmobile driving around the block?"

"Nah. What black car are you talking about?"

"Let's just wait and see if it comes back."

"All right," Tim replied as he ran off to catch another sale. While he was on his way back to John, the car rode by again. "Is that the car you're talking about?"

"Hell, yeah. That's it."

The window came rolling down as one of the men in the car stuck a shotgun out of it and fired. *BOOM! BOOM!* Shots echoed through the hood. Tranel and G Boss heard the shots and ran in the direction of the shots with guns drawn. Tranel saw the car that he had noticed earlier and fired on it. They filled the car with holes, but it managed to keep going.

"Fuck!" Tranel hollered. "Let's go see who might be hit."

G Boss and Tranel ran up the block. Samahd and BJ heard the gunshots from inside the house and ran outside to see what's going on. When BJ made it to the porch, he saw someone on the ground with a crowd lingering around.

"Come on, Samahd! Somebody's hit!"

When BJ and Samahd got there, they saw John on the ground with slugs all around his body.

"What the fuck happened!" Samahd yelled.

Everybody stood and looked on in silence. They all knew about Samahd's love for John. "Tim, go get John's car. We gotta get him to the hospital."

"The ambulance is on the way," one of the store owners informed them.

"Fuck the ambulance! He could die before it gets here!"

Tim pulled up with the door already open.

"Tim, help me get him in the car! BJ, get the car and follow us. G Boss, take all the guns and get in the car with BJ. Y'all keep an eye on us while we get him to the hospital. Move!"

When Tim got to the top of Mapes and Osbourne he noticed the same black Oldsmobile sitting in the parking lot across the street.

"Yo, Samahd! That's the car!"

Samahd rolled down the window and pointed at the car for BJ to see. Tranel jumped out of the backseat.

"Fuck that! These motherfuckas are mine."

"Back him up, BJ!" Samahd yelled out the window.

BJ pulled around them and followed Tranel. "Let's get John to the hospital. They'll handle this."

Full of rage, Tranel led the charge. The driver noticed Tranel and tried to speed off. Before they could make it to the parking lot entrance, Tranel was blocking their retreat.

"Yeah, Nigga! You thought you got away! Feel my wrath!"

The driver tried to run over Tranel, but he maneuvered to the side releasing shot after shot into the windshield. One of the bullets hit the driver in the shoulder. He swerved out of the parking lot with one hand. Out of nowhere, BJ smashed into the rear end of the car, causing it to spin out of control. The screeching of the tires didn't stop until the car crashed into another car that was sitting at the light of Shepherd and Osbourne. Tranel rushed to the car. G Boss and BJ were a few steps ahead of him. G Boss opened the car door and snatched the driver out of the car while BJ made it to the

back door and shot the backseat passenger.
Tranel pulled the passenger from the front seat.

"Who sent you?" Tranel barked.

"Fuck you, Nigga!" the battered
passenger said as he spit blood on Tranel's
shoes. "You fuckin' crab."

Tranel was so pissed off that he took the
gun by the barrel and pounded him in the face
twice before releasing three shots into his head.

"Ain't nobody left but you," G Boss said
to the driver. "Tell me who sent you and I
might let you live."

"Somebody with a lot of power and
money. You ain't seen shit yet."

"I'm ready for anything, but you won't
be around to see it." G Boss plugged three
shots into his head as well.

Samahd and Tim sat in the waiting room
of the hospital. The doctor came walking into
the emergency unit toward them.

"Excuse me, sir!" the doctor called to
Samahd.

Samahd lifted his head and rose to his
feet. "What's the word, Doc?"

"Your friend is fine. He was very lucky."

"Why is that?"

"It's obvious that he was shot with a

modified shotgun. They weren't close enough to him for the pellets to do any real damage. We pulled them out and patched him up. We gave him a shot of morphine. He should be ready to go in about six to eight hours after the morphine wears off."

"Thank you, Doc."

"That's what I'm here for. Just keep him inside for a few days to heal up."

"I'll be sure to do that."

Michelle and Donna pulled up at the house around 5:30. While they were taking the things out of the car, Donna noticed Sadeek walking up the block.

"Uggggh!" Donna growled. "Here comes Sadeek's lame ass."

"I can't stand him," Michelle remarked. "Ever since he told Samahd my business."

"Don't worry . . . I'll take care of this."

"Hey, Donna," Sadeek greeted as he approached. "Are you okay?"

"I'm fine. What do you want?"

"You must not know."

"Know what?"

"John got shot earlier today."

"What!" Donna screamed. "Who shot him?"

"I don't know. He's at Beth Israel right

now."

The two sisters jumped in the car and sped off to the hospital. Michelle and Donna rushed through the doors and to the desk.

"Excuse me, ma'am," Donna began through heavy breaths. "We're trying to find our brother."

"I'm sorry, but he's still in surgery."

"Where at, bitch? Didn't you hear me? That's my brother."

"I heard you, young lady, but you don't have to use profanity."

Samahd overheard the commotion out front and walked over to see what was going on. When he got there, he noticed that it was Donna and Michelle arguing with the lady at the desk.

"Donna!" Samahd roared. "Stop arguing with that lady and come here."

Donna snapped her head around to see who was talking to her like that. She saw that it was Samahd and calmed down immediately.

"Damn, girl. I see why you jump every time he gets mad."

"Shut up and bring your ass on." Michelle grabbed Donna by the hand and led her into the waiting room. Samahd sat them down so he could explain what was going on.

"Listen, someone came through the block

shooting, and John got hit. We don't know who because we came to the hospital with John while BJ and the rest of the guys handled the situation."

"Samahd, what is going on?" Michelle asked as she began to cry. "First you, now my brother."

"Damn it, Michelle! I don't know, but I'm going to find out before the night is over."

"How's John doing in surgery?"

"He's not in surgery. All the wounds were flesh wounds. We're just waiting for him to sober up so we can take him home. All they did was take some shotgun pellets out of his chest and patch him up."

"What do you mean all they did was take out some shotgun pellets?" Donna asked.

"Just calm down. All I'm saying is that it could've been worse than what it was."

"I'm sorry."

"Don't worry about it. I treated the doctors the same way when we got here earlier. I'm just ready to get back to the house so me and BJ can piece all of this together."

TO BE CONTINUED....

About the Author

Kareem Hicks is a native of Newark, New Jersey. He lived a life of crime and mayhem for almost 20 years until the birth of his first child in 2000. Kareem realized he had to make the best decision for his family, so with his girlfriend and new born baby they relocated to North Carolina. Kareem moved to what was a small city at the time Charlotte, NC "The Queen City". He continued in his reign over the streets of Charlotte being arrested over 10 times and incarcerated for more than 5 years in the North Carolina department of corrections. His charges ranged anywhere from possession of a weapon by convicted felon, money laundering, trafficking and attempted murder.

While incarcerated in 2009 Kareem thought to himself that maybe he should start writing about the streets instead of living them. He honestly felt he had caused too much pain and conflict and not enough love and respect. So at that moment November 10, 2009, Kareem picked up a pen bringing you his first novel of a trilogy titled "The City".

Kareem immediately worked hard to pursue his dreams of becoming a bestselling author among other urban novelist. After repeatedly contacting publishing companies time after time without any call backs, Kareem began to get frustrated. Many times he thought of returning to the streets yet he was never discouraged by his failed attempts. With the support of his family, Kareem has turned his motivation and dedication into a must read by the streets. And here lies Kareem's latest and first project "The City".